This book belongs to:

_____

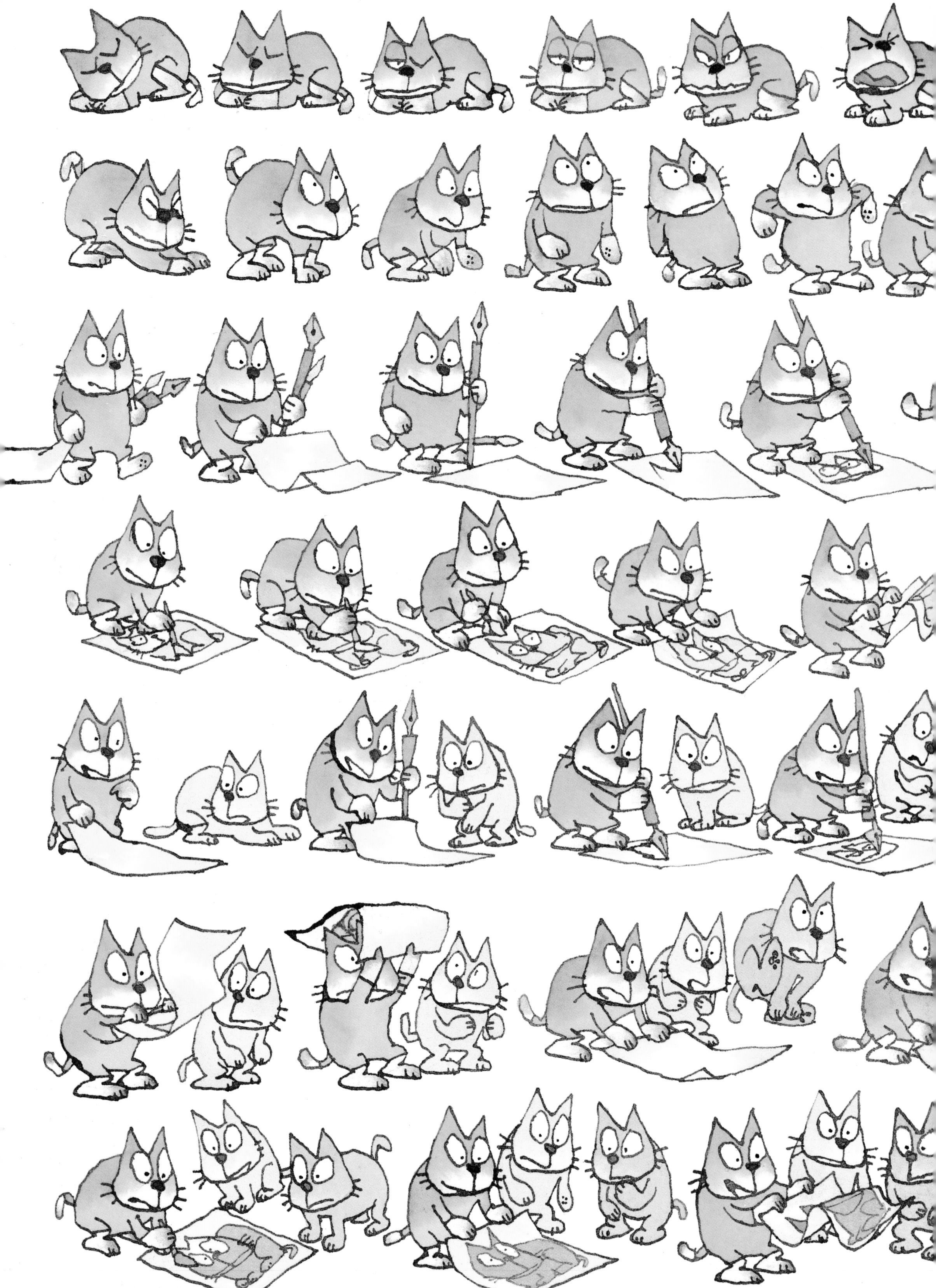

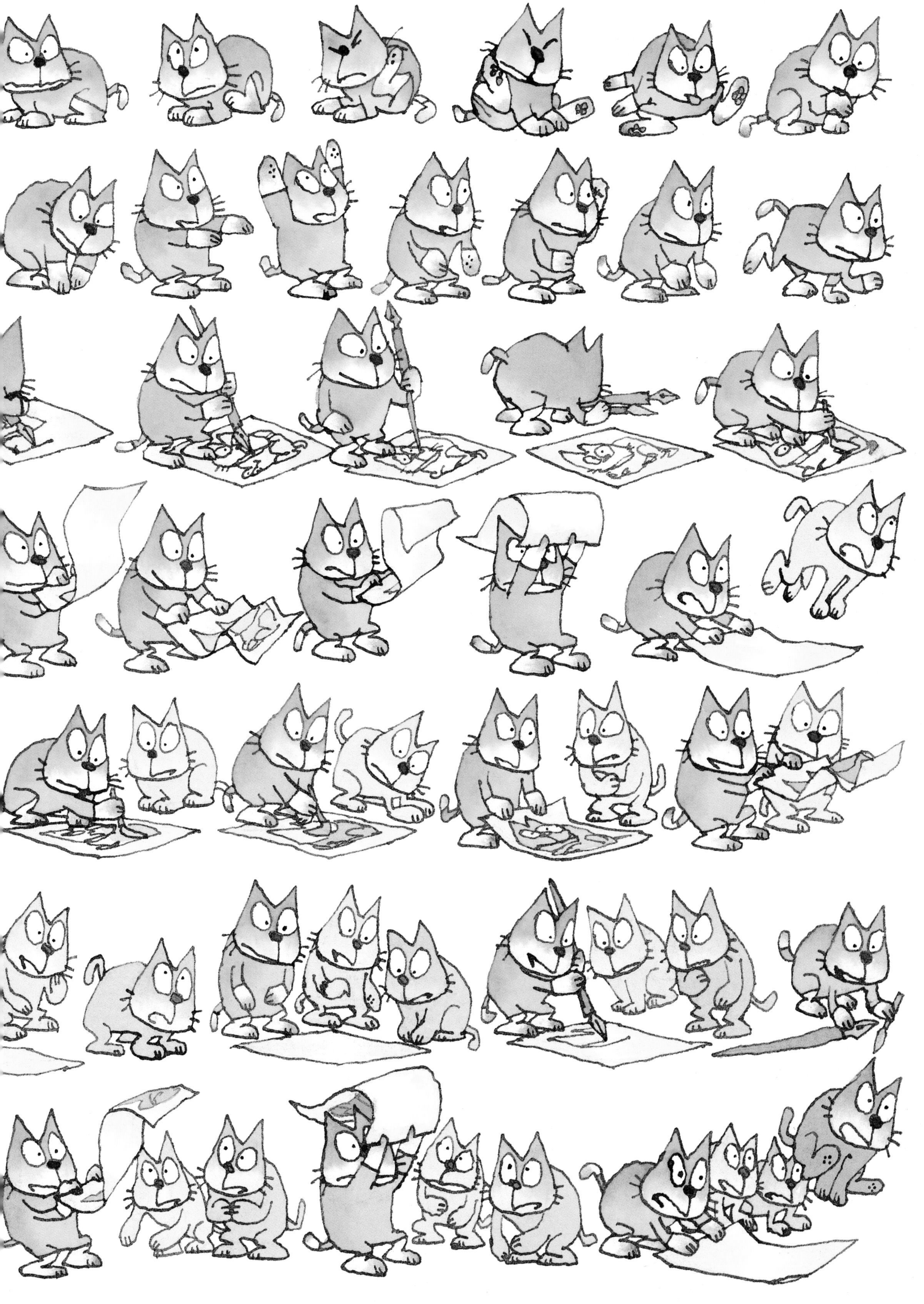

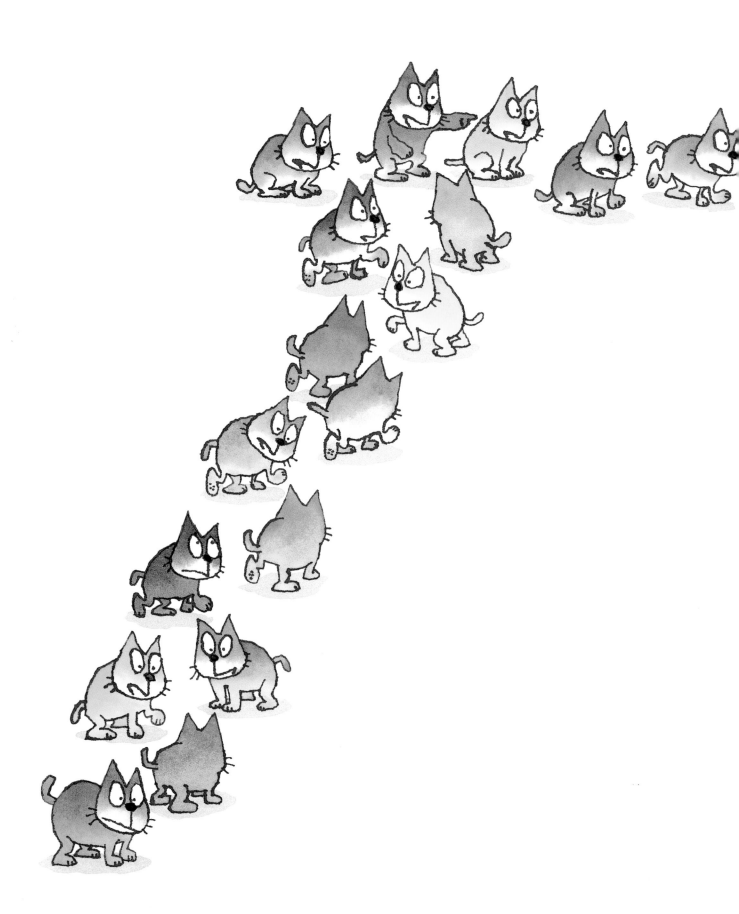

COMIC ADVENTURES OF BOOTS

This paperback edition published in 2011 by Andersen Press Ltd.
First published in Great Britain in 2002 by Andersen Press Ltd., 20 Vauxhall Bridge Road, London SW1V 2SA.
Published in Australia by Random House Australia Pty., Level 3, 100 Pacific Highway, North Sydney, NSW 2060.
Text and Illustration copyright © Satoshi Kitamura, 2002.
The rights of Satoshi Kitamura to be identified as the author and illustrator of this work
have been asserted by him in accordance with the Copyright, Designs and Patents Act, 1988.
All rights reserved. Colour separated in Switzerland by Photolitho AG, Zürich.
Printed and bound in Singapore by Tien Wah Press.

10 9 8 7 6 5 4 3 2 1

British Library Cataloguing in Publication Data available.

ISBN 978 1 84270 908 5

This book has been printed on acid-free paper

COMIC ADVENTURES OF BOOTS

SATOSHI KITAMURA

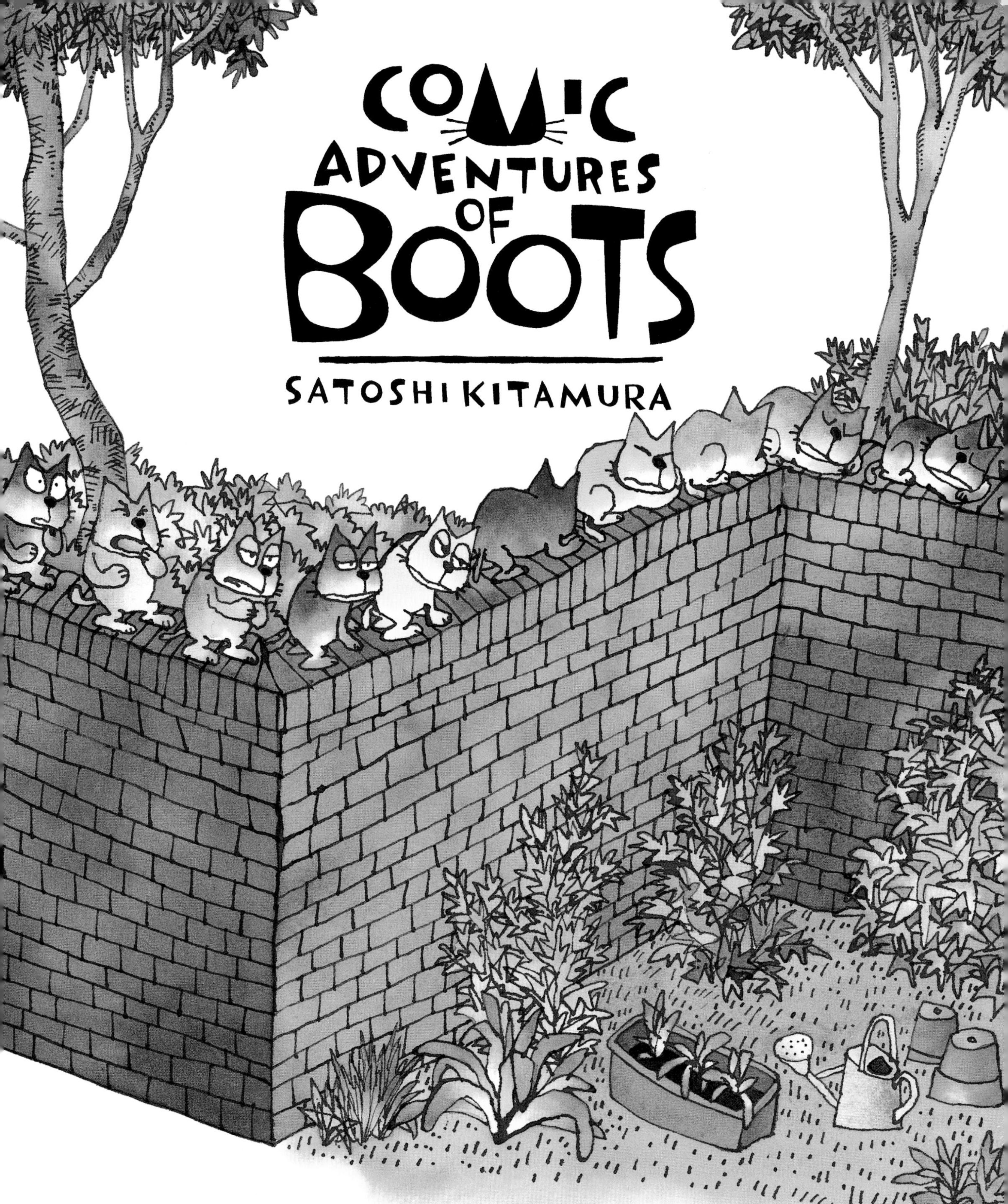

ANDERSEN PRESS
LONDON

OPERATION FISH BISCUIT

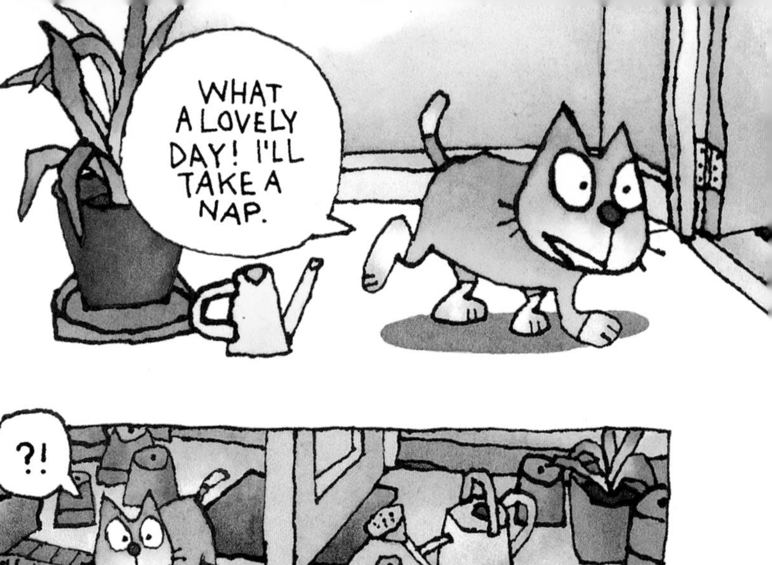

WHAT A LOVELY DAY! I'LL TAKE A NAP.

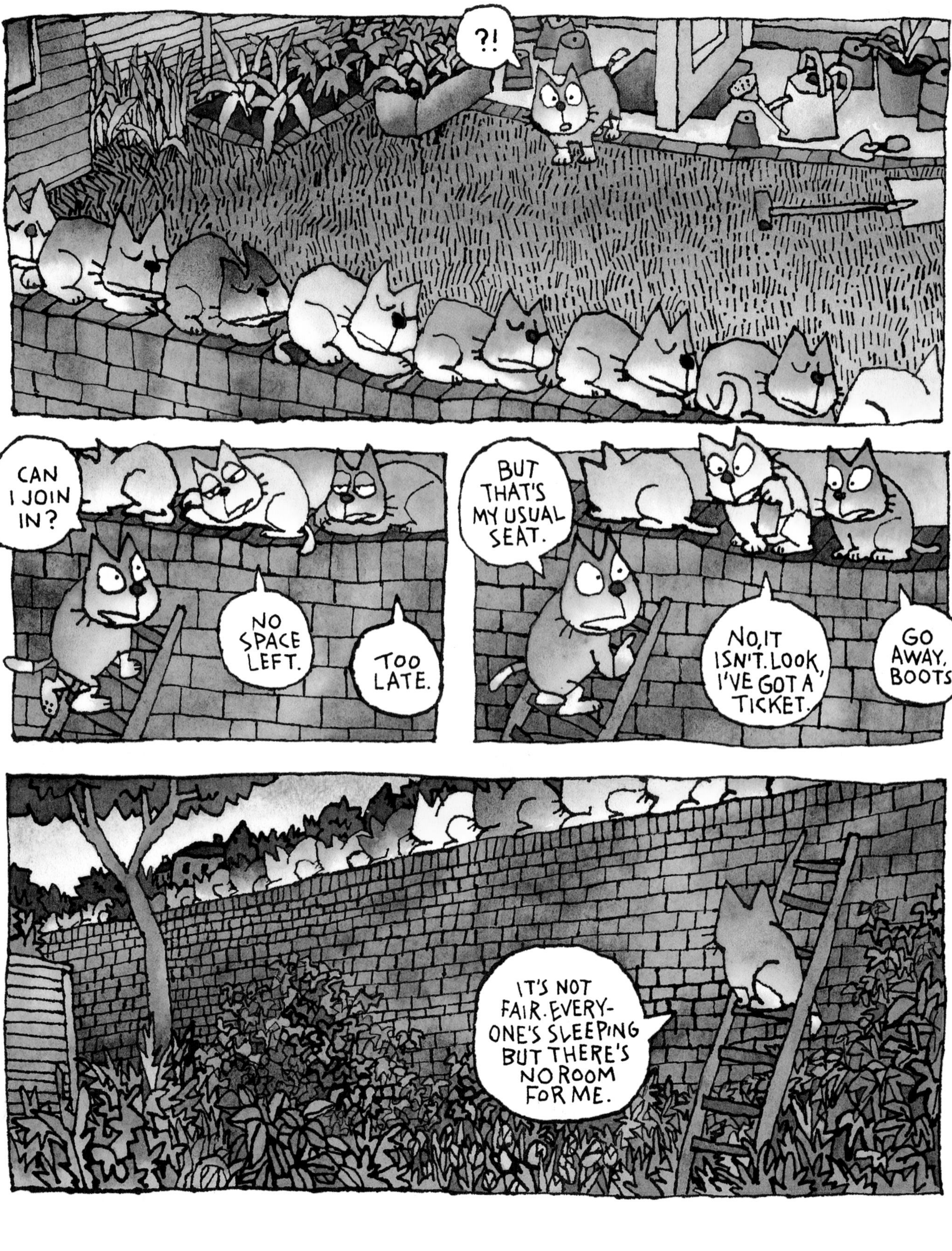

?!
CAN I JOIN IN?
NO SPACE LEFT.
TOO LATE.
BUT THAT'S MY USUAL SEAT.
NO, IT ISN'T. LOOK, I'VE GOT A TICKET.
GO AWAY, BOOTS.
IT'S NOT FAIR. EVERYONE'S SLEEPING BUT THERE'S NO ROOM FOR ME.

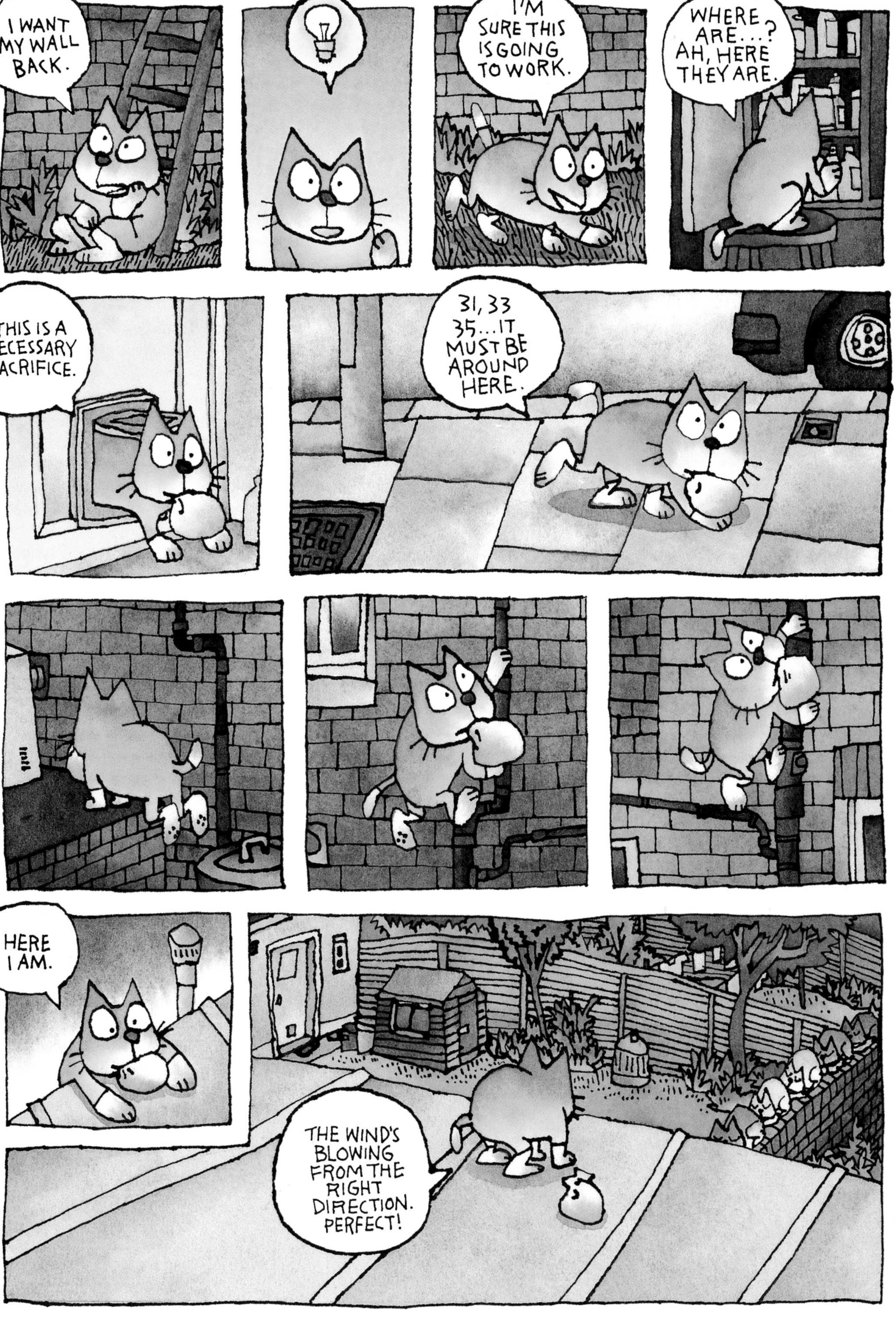
I WANT MY WALL BACK.
I'M SURE THIS IS GOING TO WORK.
WHERE ARE...? AH, HERE THEY ARE.
THIS IS A NECESSARY SACRIFICE.
31, 33 35... IT MUST BE AROUND HERE.
HERE I AM.
THE WIND'S BLOWING FROM THE RIGHT DIRECTION. PERFECT!

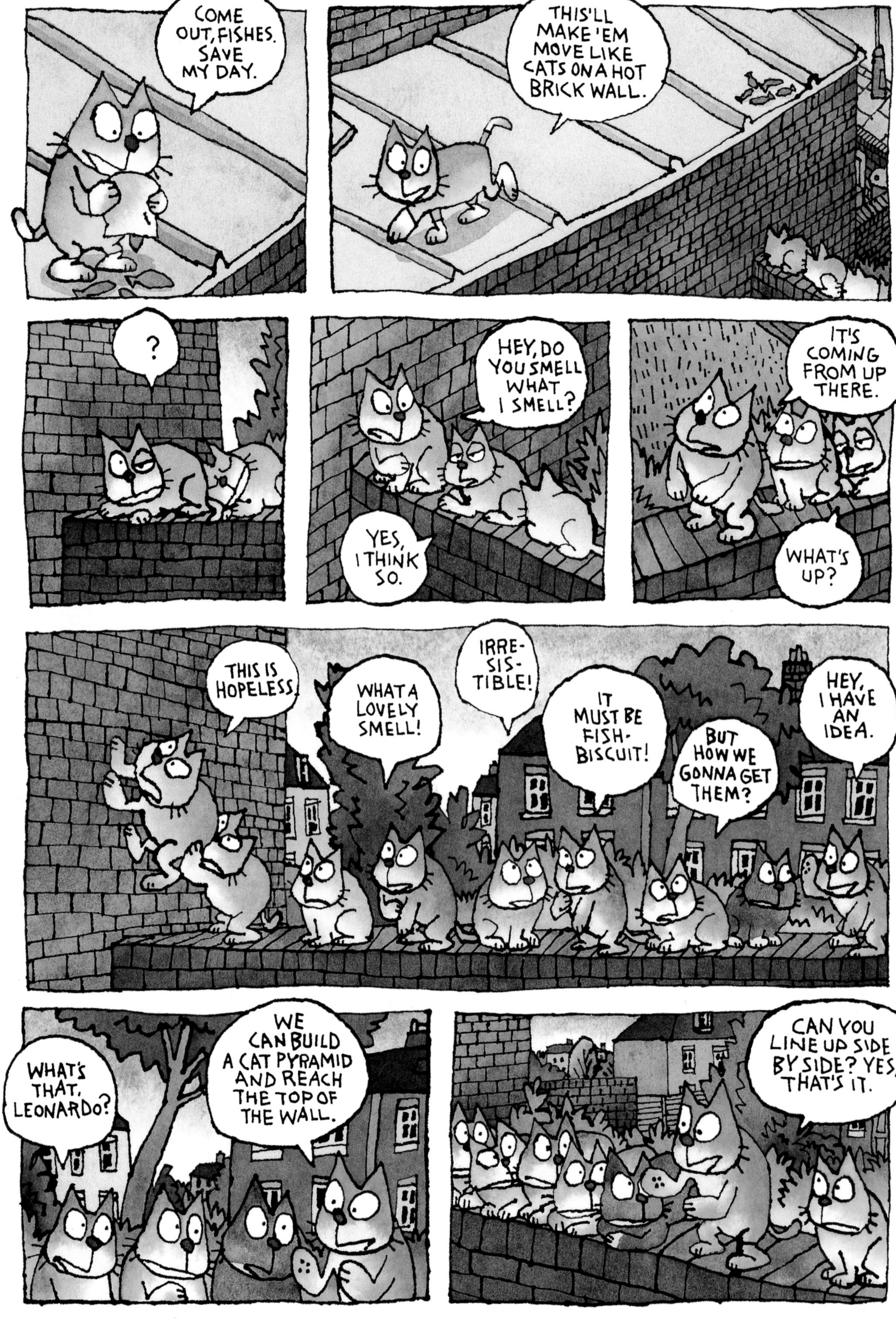
COME OUT, FISHES. SAVE MY DAY.
THIS'LL MAKE 'EM MOVE LIKE CATS ON A HOT BRICK WALL.
?
HEY, DO YOU SMELL WHAT I SMELL?
YES, I THINK SO.
IT'S COMING FROM UP THERE.
WHAT'S UP?
THIS IS HOPELESS.
WHAT A LOVELY SMELL!
IRRE-SIS-TIBLE!
IT MUST BE FISH-BISCUIT!
BUT HOW WE GONNA GET THEM?
HEY, I HAVE AN IDEA.
WHAT'S THAT, LEONARDO?
WE CAN BUILD A CAT PYRAMID AND REACH THE TOP OF THE WALL.
CAN YOU LINE UP SIDE BY SIDE? YES, THAT'S IT.

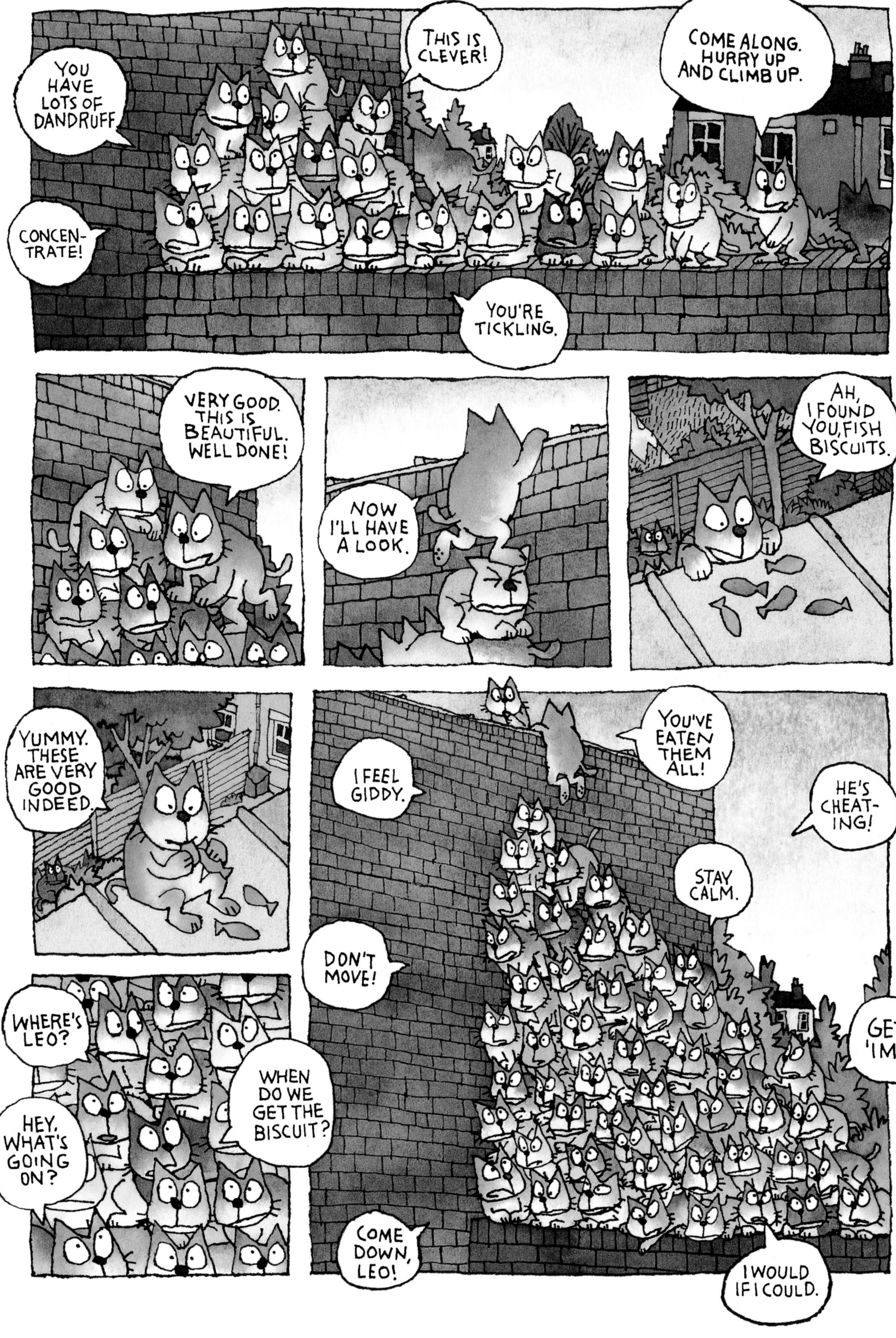
YOU HAVE LOTS OF DANDRUFF.
CONCENTRATE!
THIS IS CLEVER!
COME ALONG. HURRY UP AND CLIMB UP.
YOU'RE TICKLING.
VERY GOOD. THIS IS BEAUTIFUL. WELL DONE!
NOW I'LL HAVE A LOOK.
AH, I FOUND YOU, FISH BISCUITS.
YUMMY. THESE ARE VERY GOOD INDEED.
WHERE'S LEO?
HEY. WHAT'S GOING ON?
WHEN DO WE GET THE BISCUIT?
I FEEL GIDDY.
YOU'VE EATEN THEM ALL!
HE'S CHEATING!
STAY CALM.
DON'T MOVE!
GET 'IM!
COME DOWN, LEO!
I WOULD IF I COULD.

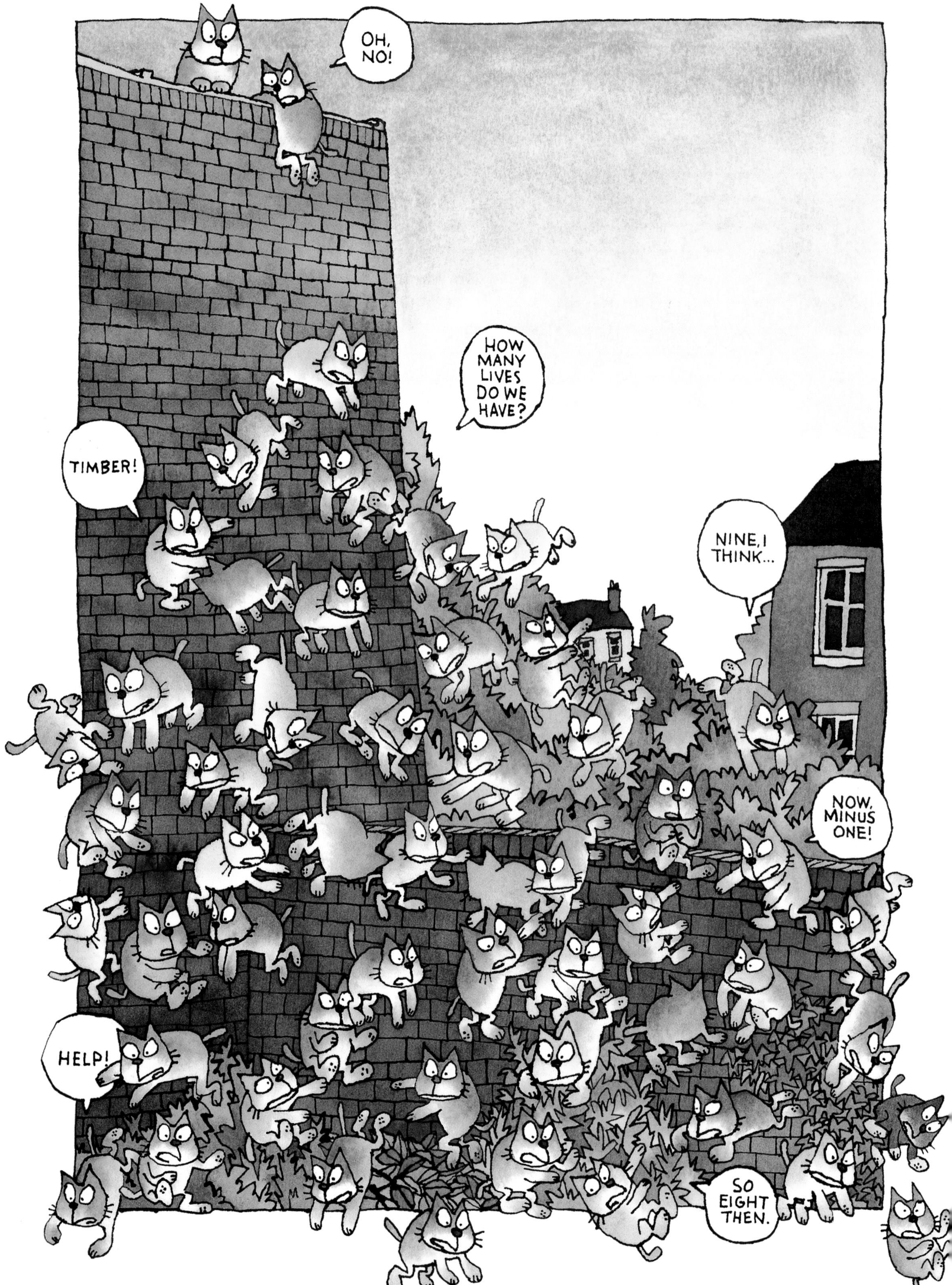
OH, NO!
HOW MANY LIVES DO WE HAVE?
TIMBER!
NINE, I THINK...
NOW, MINUS ONE!
HELP!
SO EIGHT THEN.

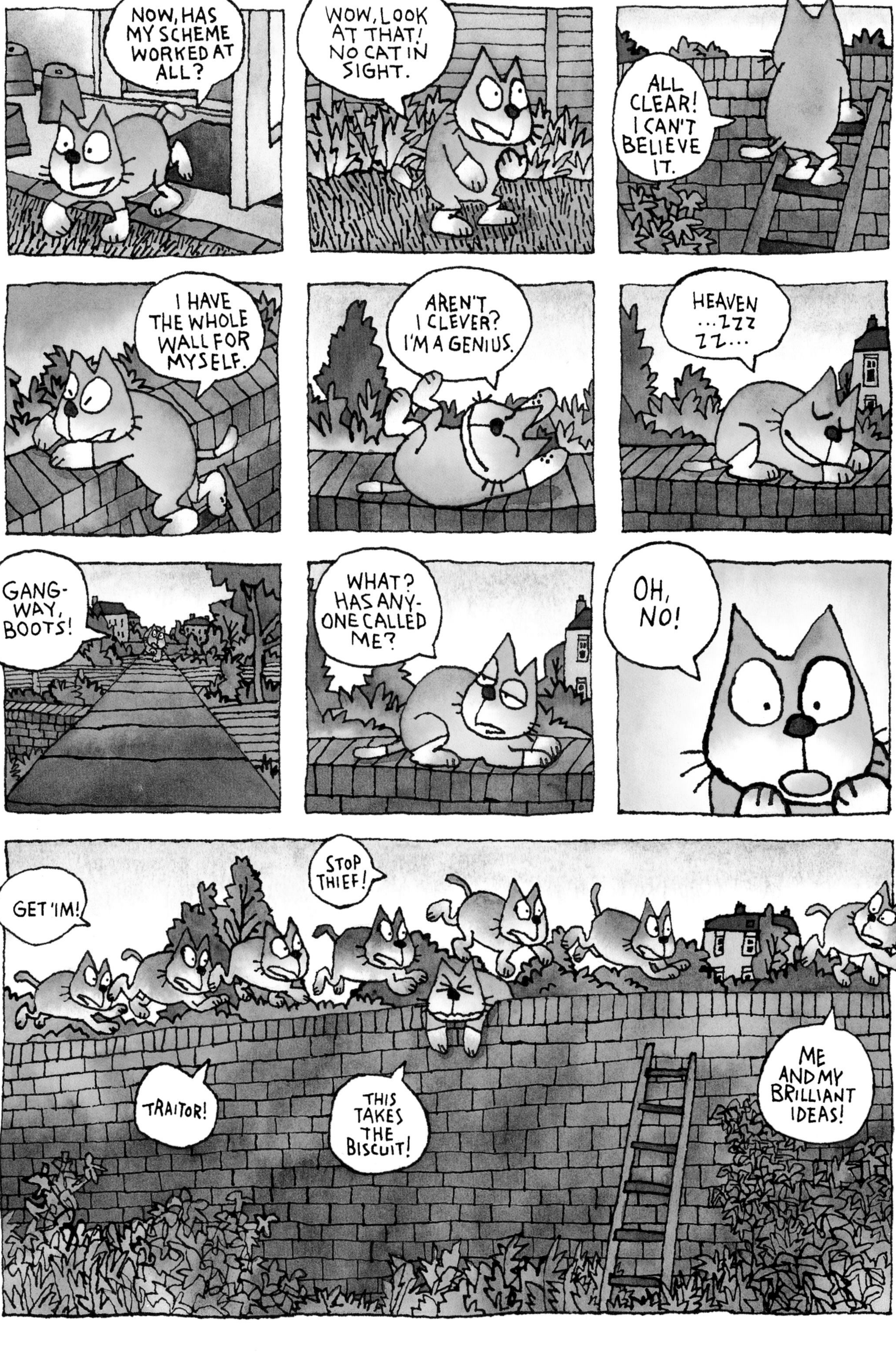
NOW, HAS MY SCHEME WORKED AT ALL?
WOW, LOOK AT THAT! NO CAT IN SIGHT.
ALL CLEAR! I CAN'T BELIEVE IT.
I HAVE THE WHOLE WALL FOR MYSELF.
AREN'T I CLEVER? I'M A GENIUS.
HEAVEN ...ZZZ ZZ...
GANG-WAY, BOOTS!
WHAT? HAS ANY-ONE CALLED ME?
OH, NO!
GET 'IM!
STOP THIEF!
TRAITOR!
THIS TAKES THE BISCUIT!
ME AND MY BRILLIANT IDEAS!

PLEASED TO MEET YOU, MADAM QUARK

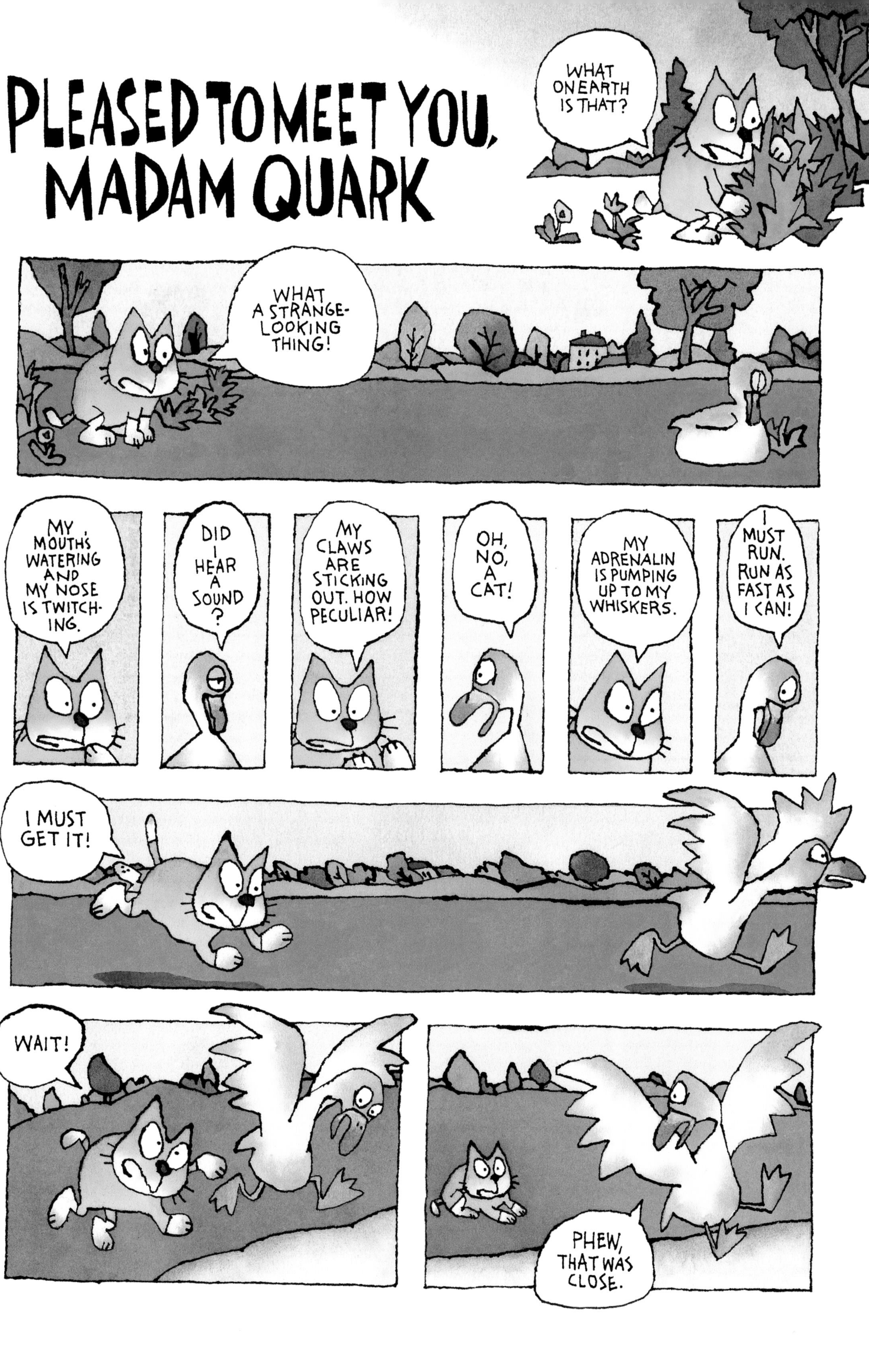
WHAT ON EARTH IS THAT?
WHAT A STRANGE-LOOKING THING!
MY MOUTH'S WATERING AND MY NOSE IS TWITCHING.
DID I HEAR A SOUND?
MY CLAWS ARE STICKING OUT. HOW PECULIAR!
OH, NO, A CAT!
MY ADRENALIN IS PUMPING UP TO MY WHISKERS.
I MUST RUN. RUN AS FAST AS I CAN!
I MUST GET IT!
WAIT!
PHEW, THAT WAS CLOSE.

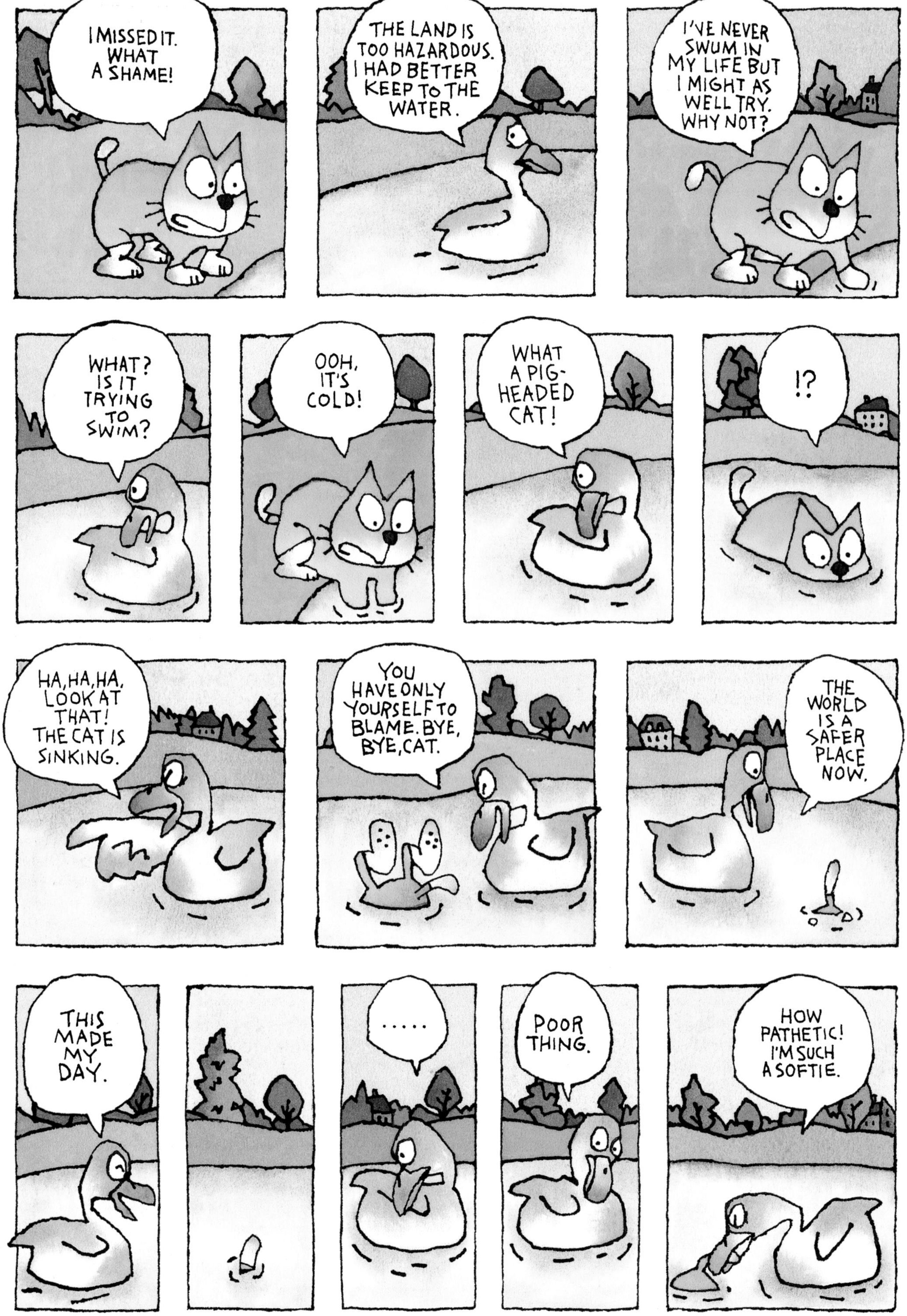
I MISSED IT. WHAT A SHAME!
THE LAND IS TOO HAZARDOUS. I HAD BETTER KEEP TO THE WATER.
I'VE NEVER SWUM IN MY LIFE BUT I MIGHT AS WELL TRY. WHY NOT?
WHAT? IS IT TRYING TO SWIM?
OOH, IT'S COLD!
WHAT A PIG-HEADED CAT!
!?
HA, HA, HA, LOOK AT THAT! THE CAT IS SINKING.
YOU HAVE ONLY YOURSELF TO BLAME. BYE, BYE, CAT.
THE WORLD IS A SAFER PLACE NOW.
THIS MADE MY DAY.
......
POOR THING.
HOW PATHETIC! I'M SUCH A SOFTIE.

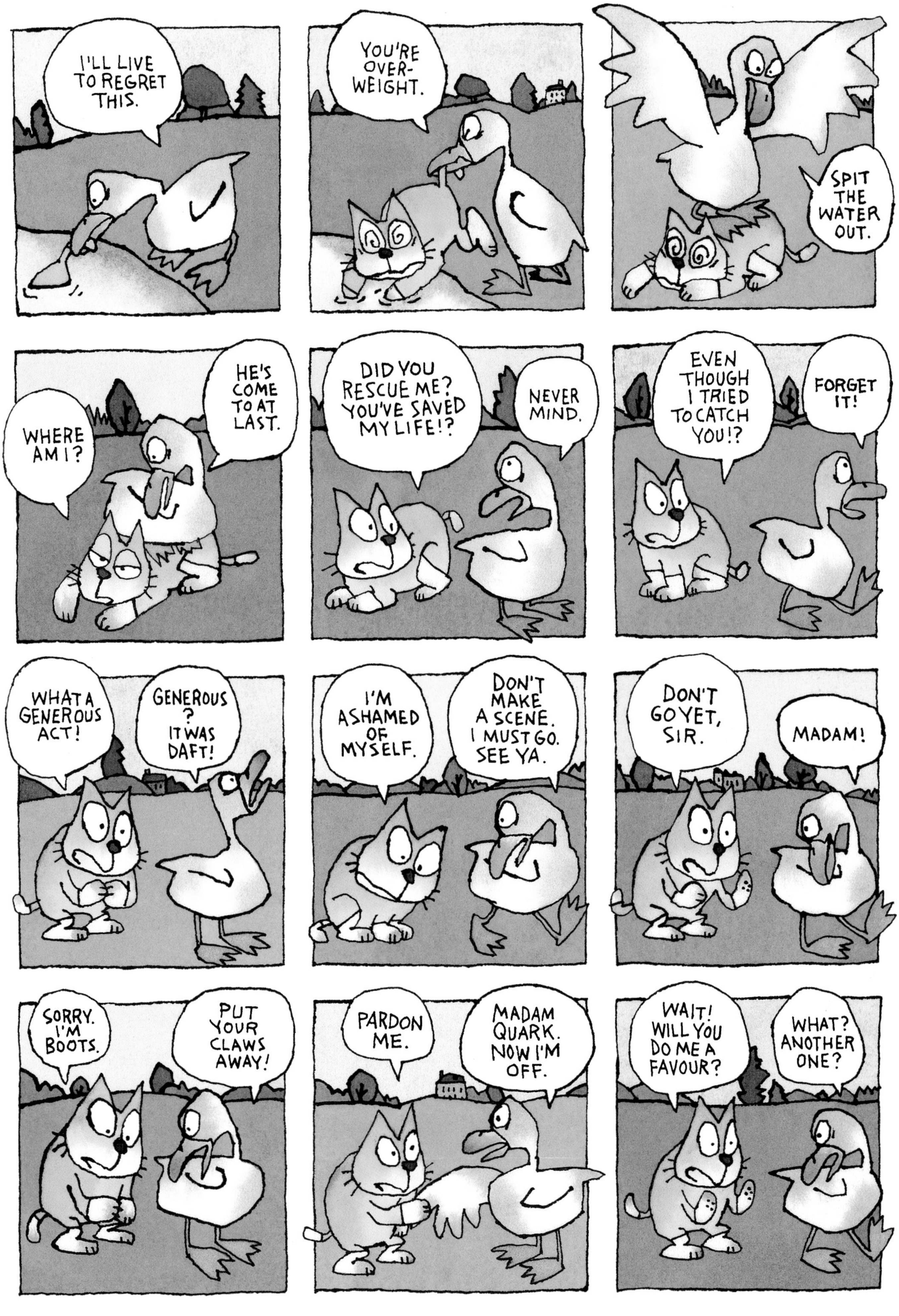
I'LL LIVE TO REGRET THIS.
YOU'RE OVER-WEIGHT.
SPIT THE WATER OUT.
WHERE AM I?
HE'S COME TO AT LAST.
DID YOU RESCUE ME? YOU'VE SAVED MY LIFE!?
NEVER MIND.
EVEN THOUGH I TRIED TO CATCH YOU!?
FORGET IT!
WHAT A GENEROUS ACT!
GENEROUS? IT WAS DAFT!
I'M ASHAMED OF MYSELF.
DON'T MAKE A SCENE. I MUST GO. SEE YA.
DON'T GO YET, SIR.
MADAM!
SORRY. I'M BOOTS.
PUT YOUR CLAWS AWAY!
PARDON ME.
MADAM QUARK. NOW I'M OFF.
WAIT! WILL YOU DO ME A FAVOUR?
WHAT? ANOTHER ONE?

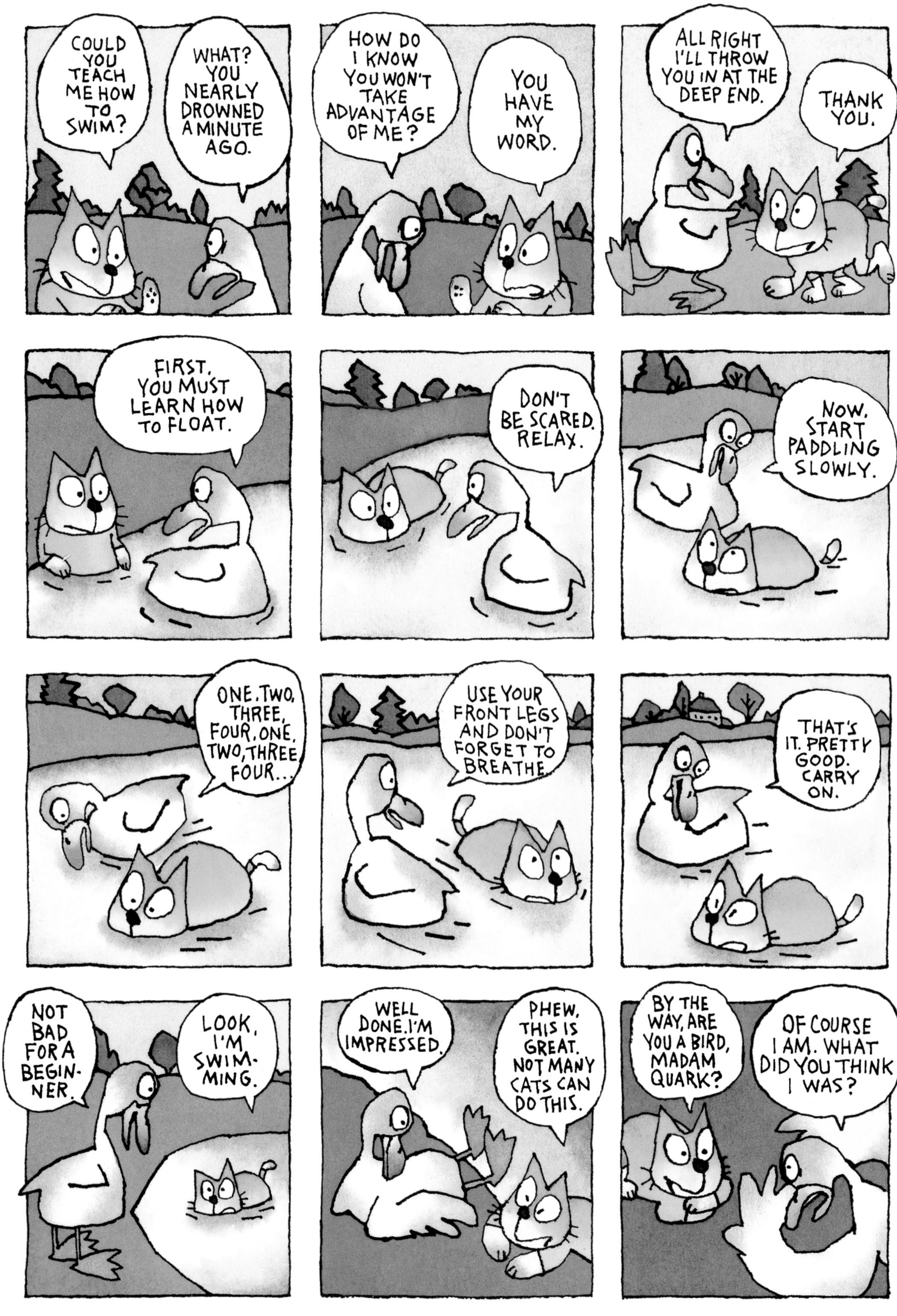
COULD YOU TEACH ME HOW TO SWIM?
WHAT? YOU NEARLY DROWNED A MINUTE AGO.
HOW DO I KNOW YOU WON'T TAKE ADVANTAGE OF ME?
YOU HAVE MY WORD.
ALL RIGHT I'LL THROW YOU IN AT THE DEEP END.
THANK YOU.
FIRST, YOU MUST LEARN HOW TO FLOAT.
DON'T BE SCARED. RELAX.
NOW, START PADDLING SLOWLY.
ONE, TWO, THREE, FOUR, ONE, TWO, THREE FOUR...
USE YOUR FRONT LEGS AND DON'T FORGET TO BREATHE.
THAT'S IT. PRETTY GOOD. CARRY ON.
NOT BAD FOR A BEGINNER.
LOOK, I'M SWIMMING.
WELL DONE. I'M IMPRESSED.
PHEW, THIS IS GREAT. NOT MANY CATS CAN DO THIS.
BY THE WAY, ARE YOU A BIRD, MADAM QUARK?
OF COURSE I AM. WHAT DID YOU THINK I WAS?

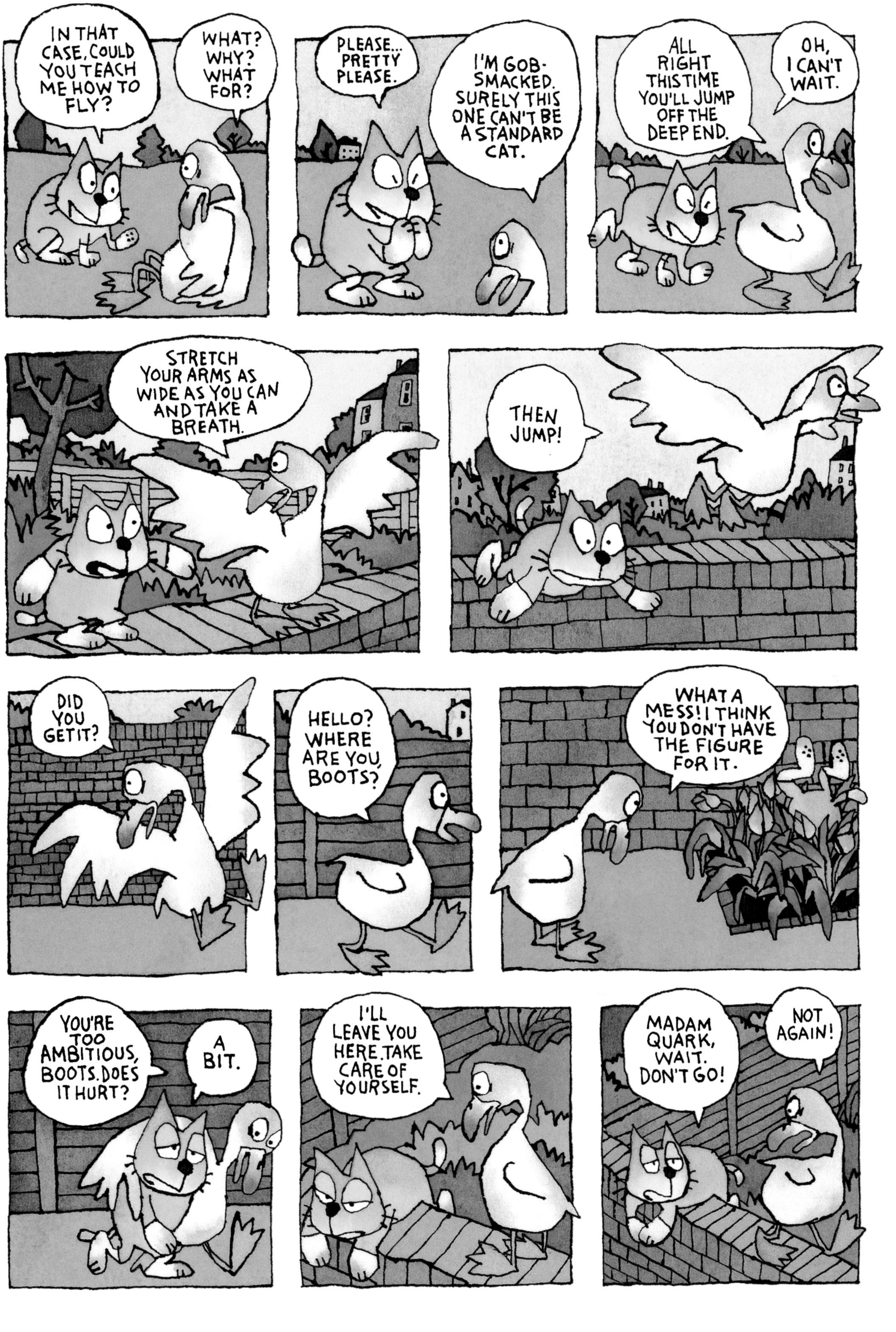
IN THAT CASE, COULD YOU TEACH ME HOW TO FLY?
WHAT? WHY? WHAT FOR?
PLEASE... PRETTY PLEASE.
I'M GOB-SMACKED. SURELY THIS ONE CAN'T BE A STANDARD CAT.
ALL RIGHT THIS TIME YOU'LL JUMP OFF THE DEEP END.
OH, I CAN'T WAIT.
STRETCH YOUR ARMS AS WIDE AS YOU CAN AND TAKE A BREATH.
THEN JUMP!
DID YOU GET IT?
HELLO? WHERE ARE YOU, BOOTS?
WHAT A MESS! I THINK YOU DON'T HAVE THE FIGURE FOR IT.
YOU'RE TOO AMBITIOUS, BOOTS. DOES IT HURT?
A BIT.
I'LL LEAVE YOU HERE. TAKE CARE OF YOURSELF.
MADAM QUARK, WAIT. DON'T GO!
NOT AGAIN!

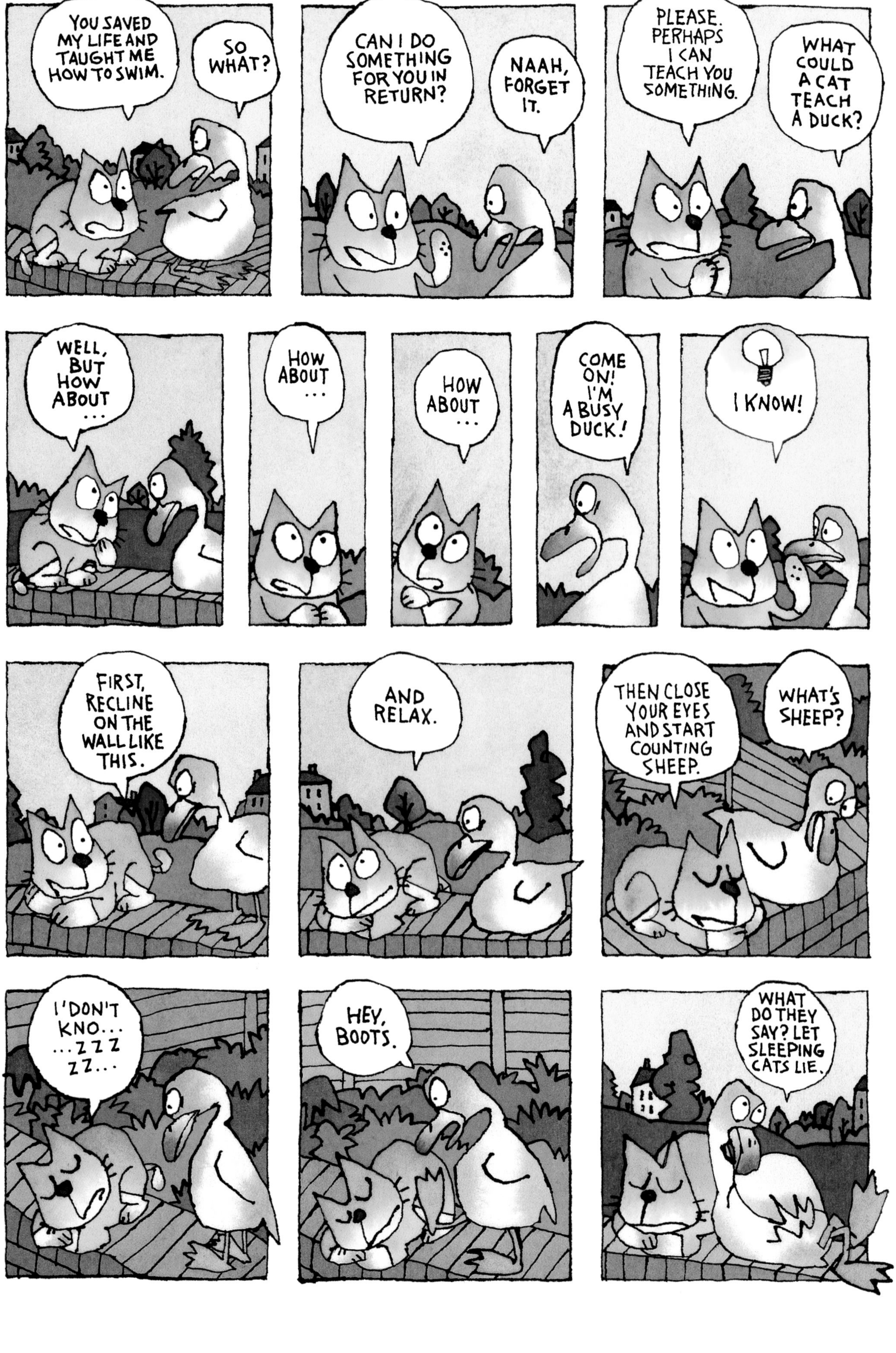
YOU SAVED MY LIFE AND TAUGHT ME HOW TO SWIM.
SO WHAT?
CAN I DO SOMETHING FOR YOU IN RETURN?
NAAH, FORGET IT.
PLEASE. PERHAPS I CAN TEACH YOU SOMETHING.
WHAT COULD A CAT TEACH A DUCK?
WELL, BUT HOW ABOUT ...
HOW ABOUT ...
HOW ABOUT ...
COME ON! I'M A BUSY DUCK!
I KNOW!
FIRST, RECLINE ON THE WALL LIKE THIS.
AND RELAX.
THEN CLOSE YOUR EYES AND START COUNTING SHEEP.
WHAT'S SHEEP?
I'DON'T KNO... ...ZZZ ZZ...
HEY, BOOTS.
WHAT DO THEY SAY? LET SLEEPING CATS LIE.

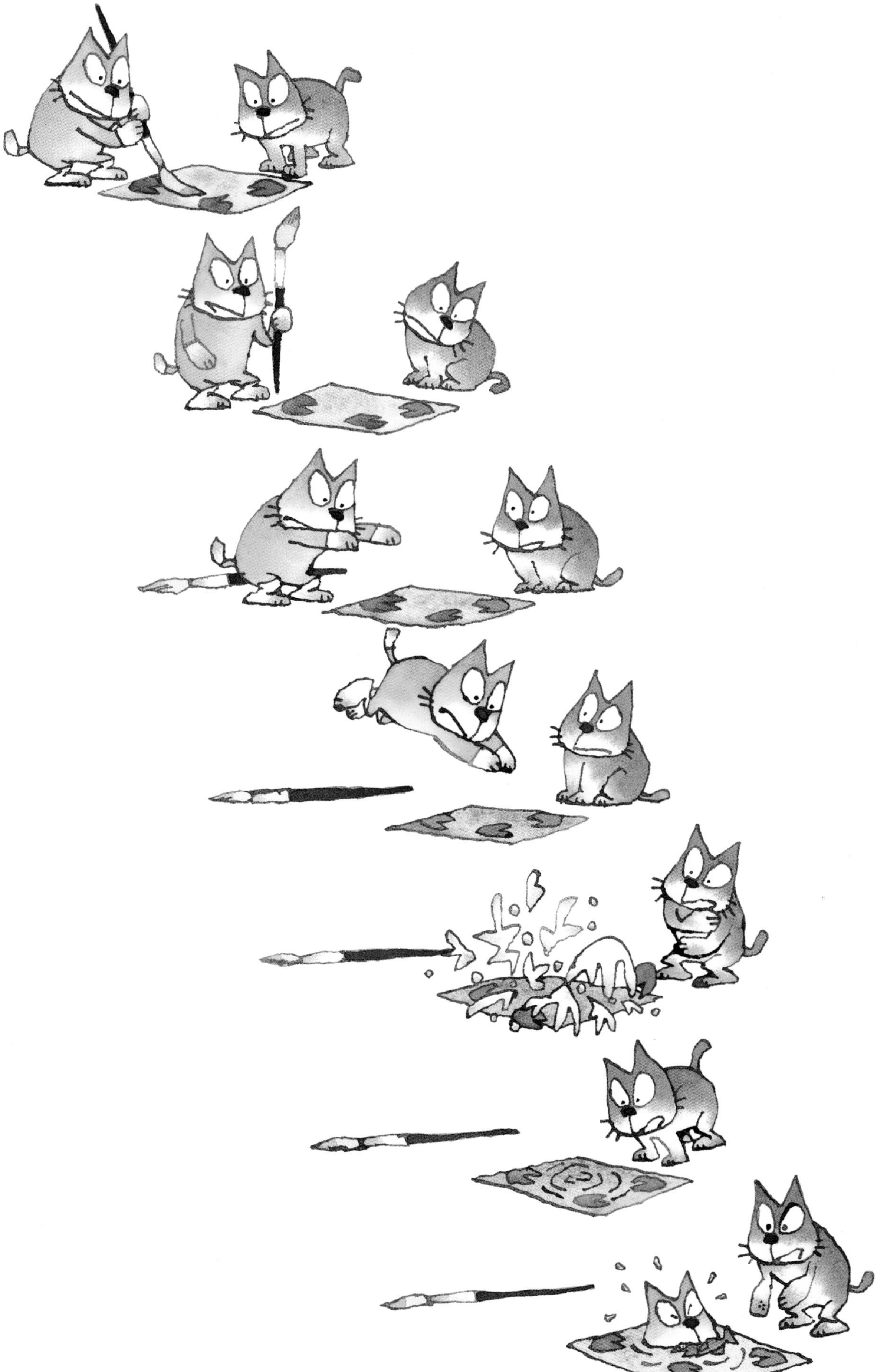

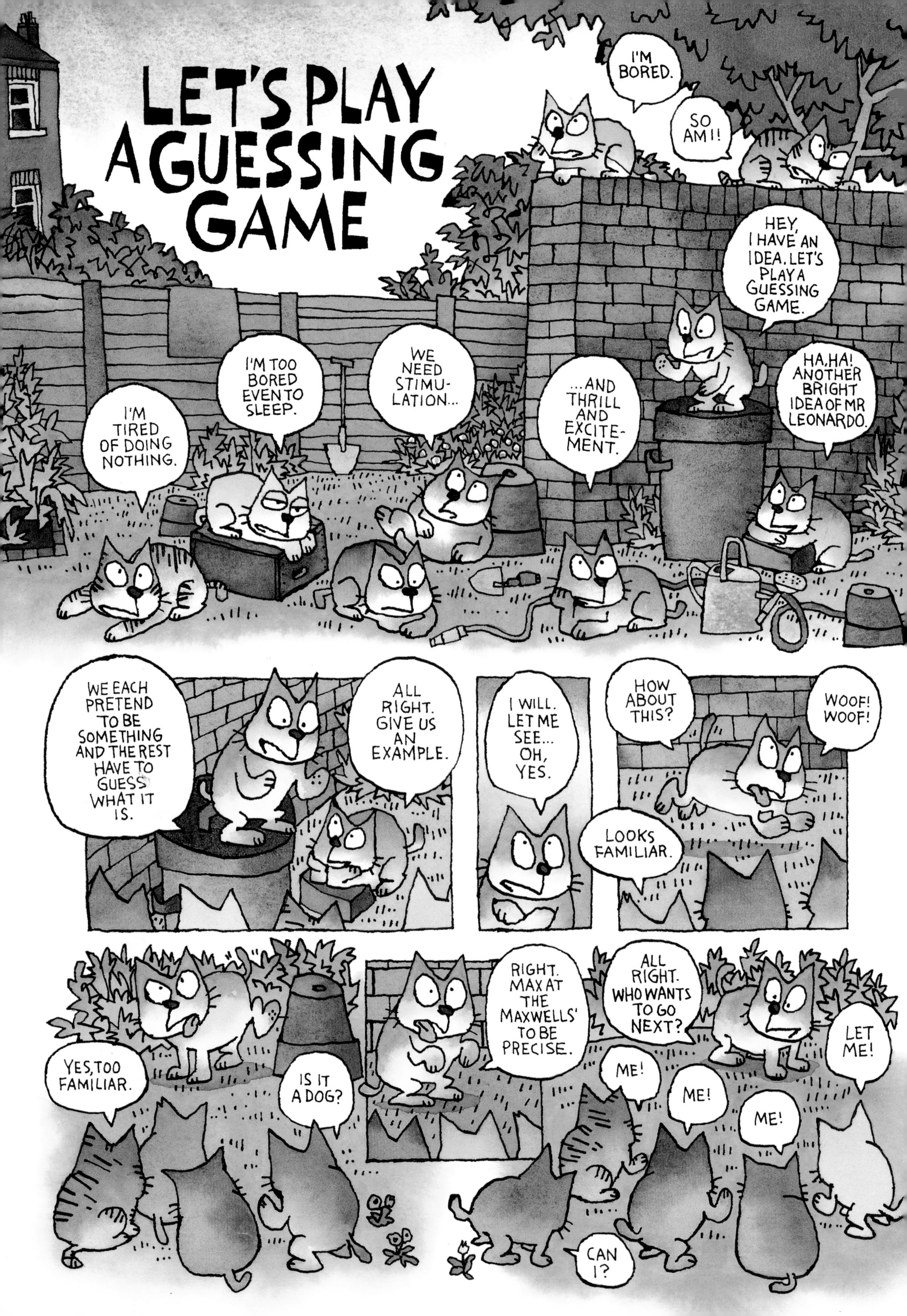
LET'S PLAY A GUESSING GAME
I'M BORED.
SO AM I!
HEY, I HAVE AN IDEA. LET'S PLAY A GUESSING GAME.
I'M TIRED OF DOING NOTHING.
I'M TOO BORED EVEN TO SLEEP.
WE NEED STIMU-LATION...
...AND THRILL AND EXCITE-MENT.
HA, HA! ANOTHER BRIGHT IDEA OF MR LEONARDO.
WE EACH PRETEND TO BE SOMETHING AND THE REST HAVE TO GUESS WHAT IT IS.
ALL RIGHT. GIVE US AN EXAMPLE.
I WILL. LET ME SEE... OH, YES.
HOW ABOUT THIS?
WOOF! WOOF!
LOOKS FAMILIAR.
YES, TOO FAMILIAR.
IS IT A DOG?
RIGHT. MAX AT THE MAXWELLS' TO BE PRECISE.
ALL RIGHT. WHO WANTS TO GO NEXT?
ME!
ME!
ME!
LET ME!
CAN I?

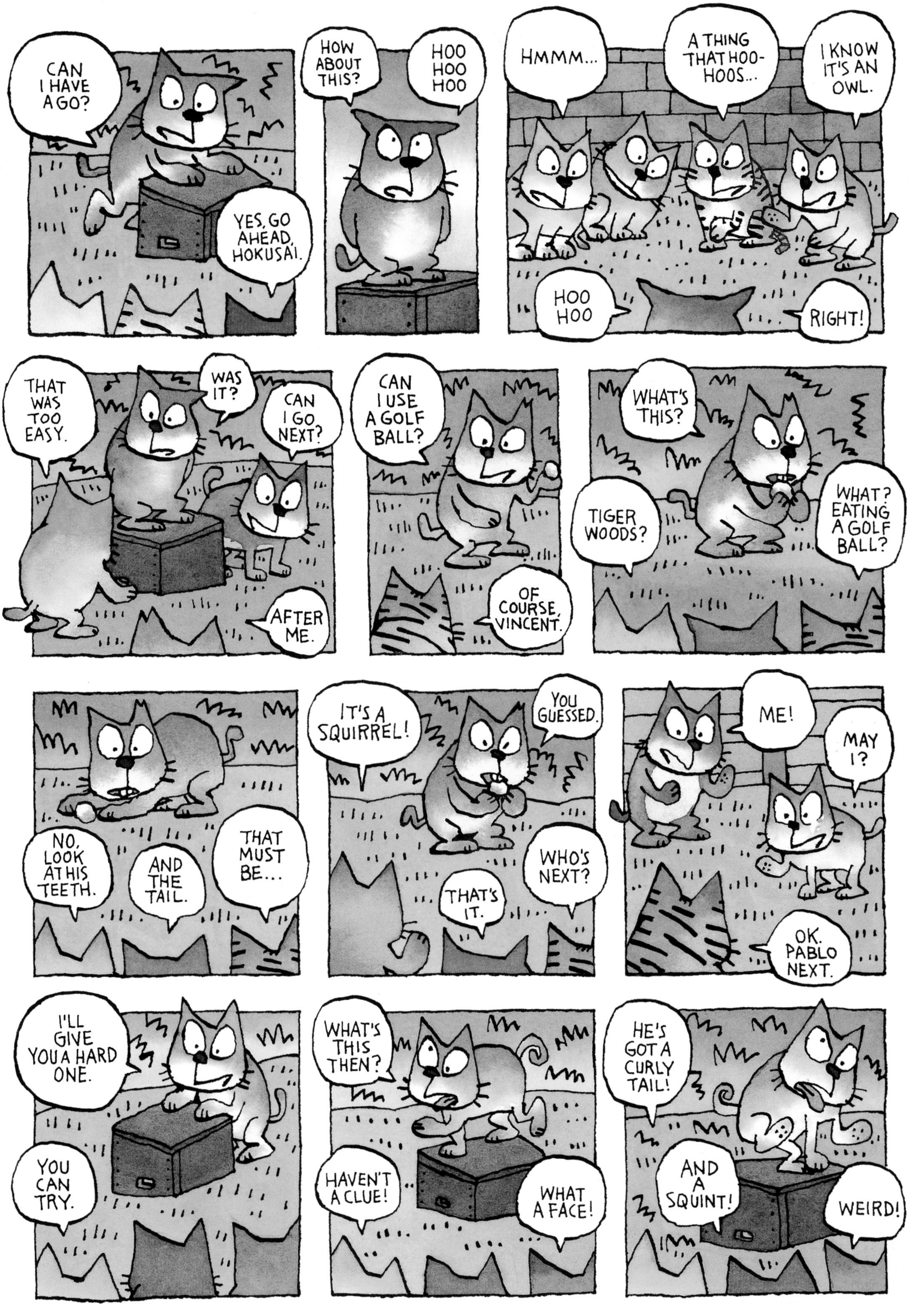
CAN I HAVE A GO?
YES, GO AHEAD, HOKUSAI.
HOW ABOUT THIS?
HOO HOO HOO
HMMM...
A THING THAT HOO-HOOS...
I KNOW IT'S AN OWL.
HOO HOO
RIGHT!
THAT WAS TOO EASY.
WAS IT?
CAN I GO NEXT?
AFTER ME.
CAN I USE A GOLF BALL?
OF COURSE, VINCENT.
WHAT'S THIS?
TIGER WOODS?
WHAT? EATING A GOLF BALL?
NO, LOOK AT HIS TEETH.
AND THE TAIL.
THAT MUST BE...
IT'S A SQUIRREL!
YOU GUESSED.
THAT'S IT.
WHO'S NEXT?
ME!
MAY I?
OK. PABLO NEXT.
I'LL GIVE YOU A HARD ONE.
YOU CAN TRY.
WHAT'S THIS THEN?
HAVEN'T A CLUE!
WHAT A FACE!
HE'S GOT A CURLY TAIL!
AND A SQUINT!
WEIRD!

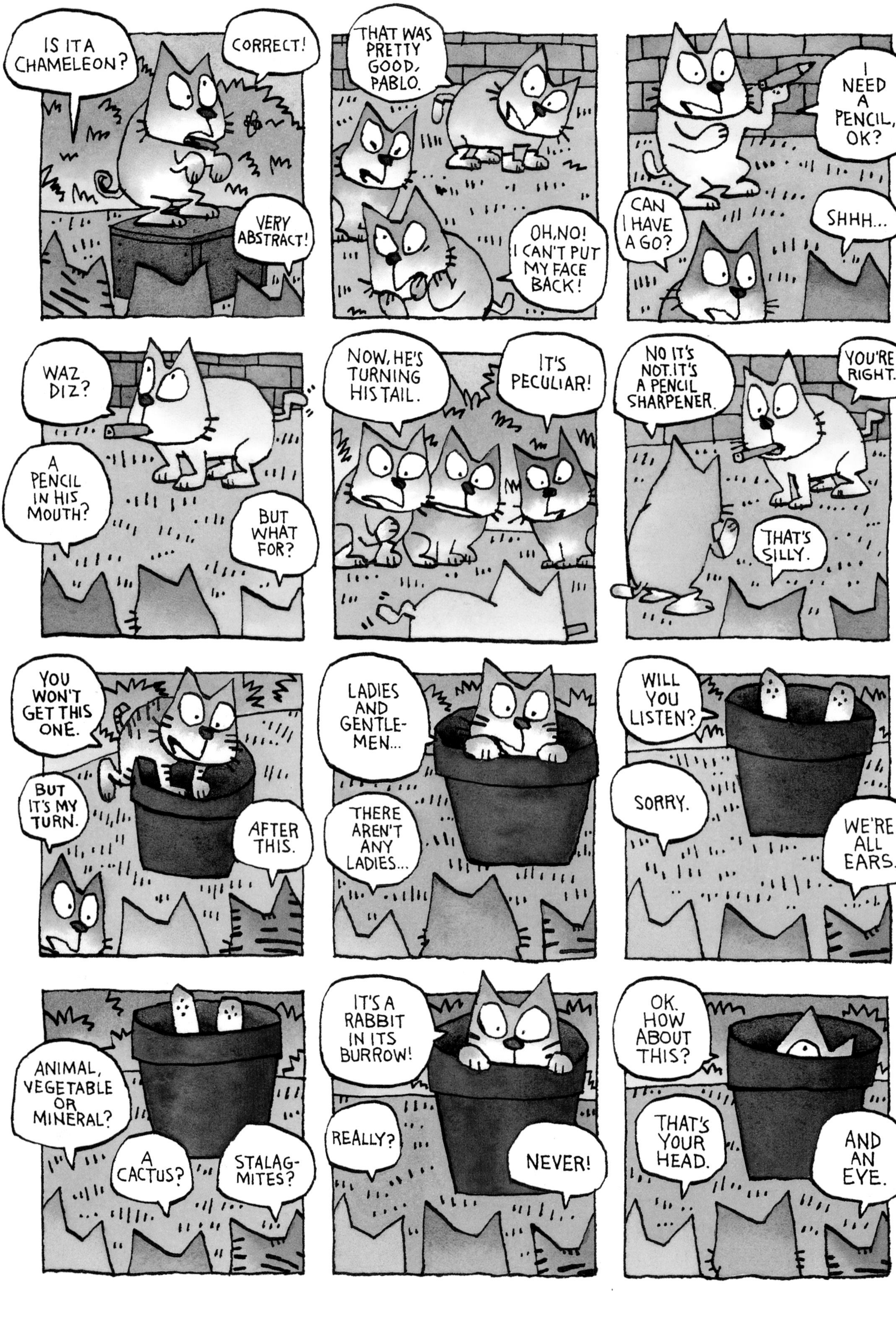

IS IT A CHAMELEON?
CORRECT!
VERY ABSTRACT!
THAT WAS PRETTY GOOD, PABLO.
OH, NO! I CAN'T PUT MY FACE BACK!
I NEED A PENCIL, OK?
CAN I HAVE A GO?
SHHH...
WAZ DIZ?
A PENCIL IN HIS MOUTH?
BUT WHAT FOR?
NOW, HE'S TURNING HIS TAIL.
IT'S PECULIAR!
NO IT'S NOT. IT'S A PENCIL SHARPENER.
YOU'RE RIGHT.
THAT'S SILLY.
YOU WON'T GET THIS ONE.
BUT IT'S MY TURN.
AFTER THIS.
LADIES AND GENTLE-MEN...
THERE AREN'T ANY LADIES...
WILL YOU LISTEN?
SORRY.
WE'RE ALL EARS.
ANIMAL, VEGETABLE OR MINERAL?
A CACTUS?
STALAG-MITES?
IT'S A RABBIT IN ITS BURROW!
REALLY?
NEVER!
OK. HOW ABOUT THIS?
THAT'S YOUR HEAD.
AND AN EYE.

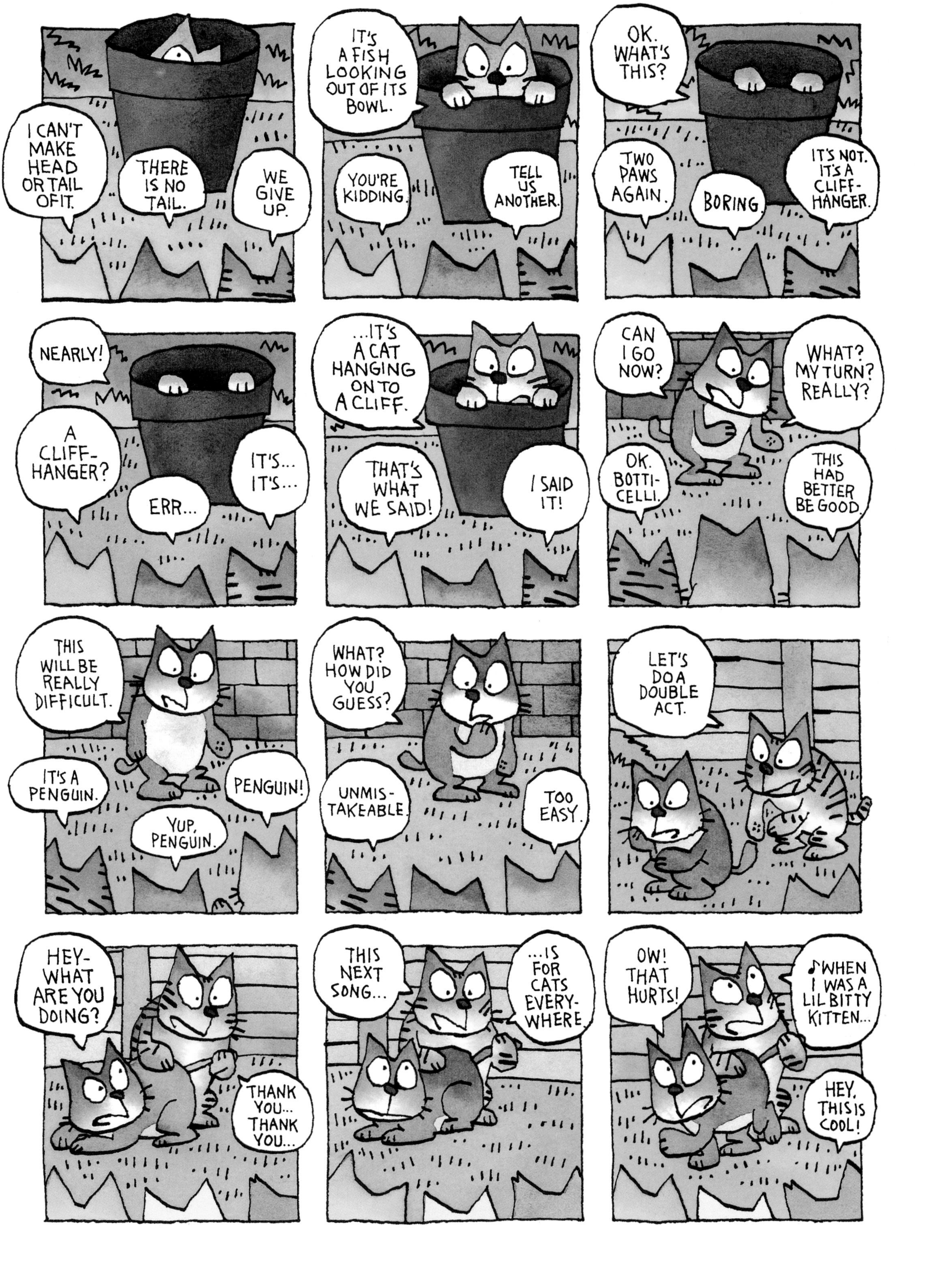
I CAN'T MAKE HEAD OR TAIL OF IT.
THERE IS NO TAIL.
WE GIVE UP.
IT'S A FISH LOOKING OUT OF ITS BOWL.
YOU'RE KIDDING.
TELL US ANOTHER.
OK. WHAT'S THIS?
TWO PAWS AGAIN.
BORING.
IT'S NOT. IT'S A CLIFF-HANGER.
NEARLY!
A CLIFF-HANGER?
ERR...
IT'S... IT'S...
...IT'S A CAT HANGING ON TO A CLIFF.
THAT'S WHAT WE SAID!
I SAID IT!
CAN I GO NOW?
WHAT? MY TURN? REALLY?
OK. BOTTI-CELLI.
THIS HAD BETTER BE GOOD.
THIS WILL BE REALLY DIFFICULT.
IT'S A PENGUIN.
YUP, PENGUIN.
PENGUIN!
WHAT? HOW DID YOU GUESS?
UNMIS-TAKEABLE.
TOO EASY.
LET'S DO A DOUBLE ACT.
HEY-WHAT ARE YOU DOING?
THANK YOU... THANK YOU...
THIS NEXT SONG...
...IS FOR CATS EVERY-WHERE.
OW! THAT HURTS!
♪WHEN I WAS A LIL BITTY KITTEN...
HEY, THIS IS COOL!

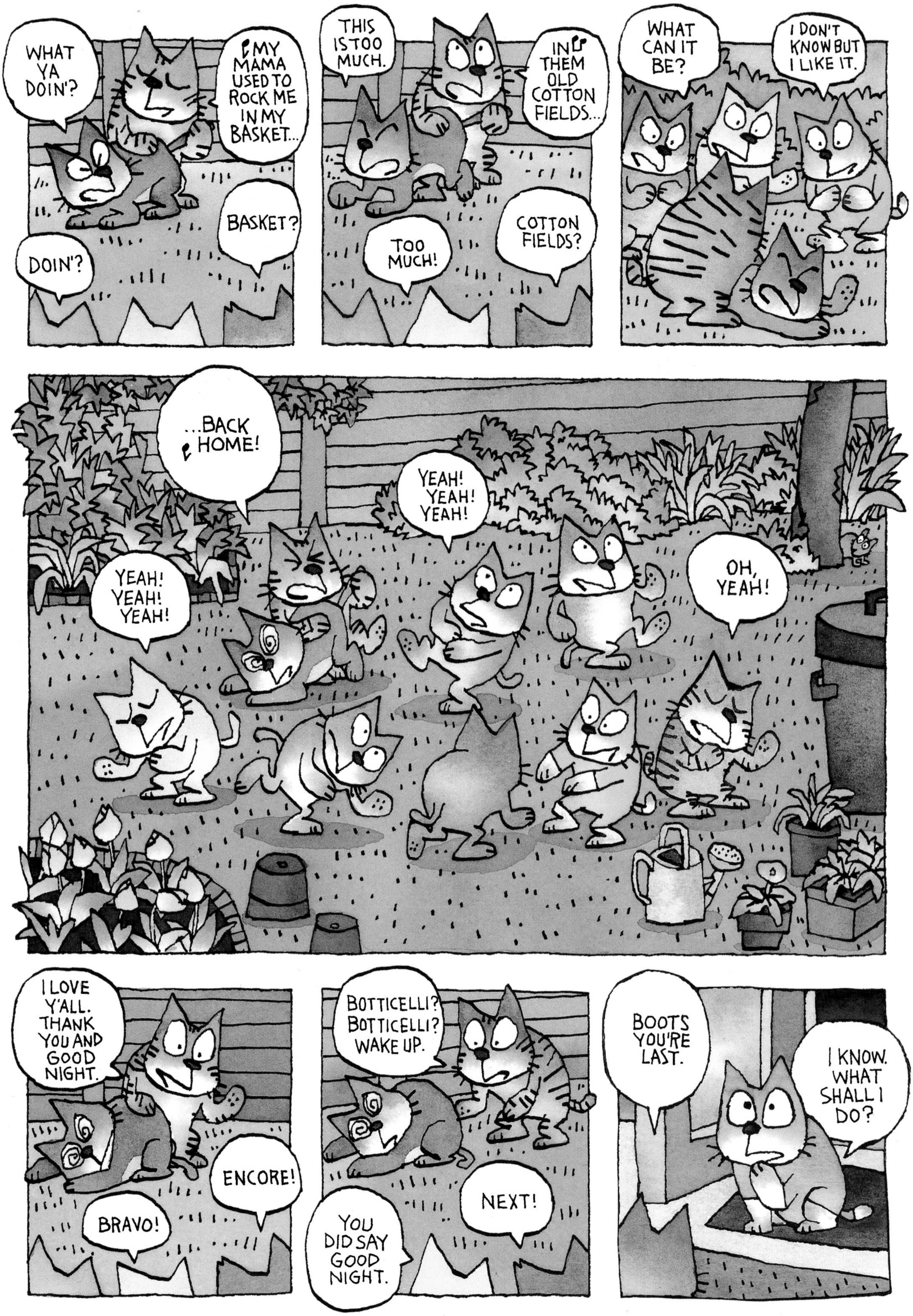

WHAT YA DOIN'?
MY MAMA USED TO ROCK ME IN MY BASKET...
DOIN'?
BASKET?
THIS IS TOO MUCH.
IN THEM OLD COTTON FIELDS...
TOO MUCH!
COTTON FIELDS?
WHAT CAN IT BE?
I DON'T KNOW BUT I LIKE IT.
...BACK HOME!
YEAH! YEAH! YEAH!
YEAH! YEAH! YEAH!
OH, YEAH!
I LOVE Y'ALL. THANK YOU AND GOOD NIGHT.
ENCORE!
BRAVO!
BOTTICELLI? BOTTICELLI? WAKE UP.
NEXT!
YOU DID SAY GOOD NIGHT.
BOOTS YOU'RE LAST.
I KNOW. WHAT SHALL I DO?

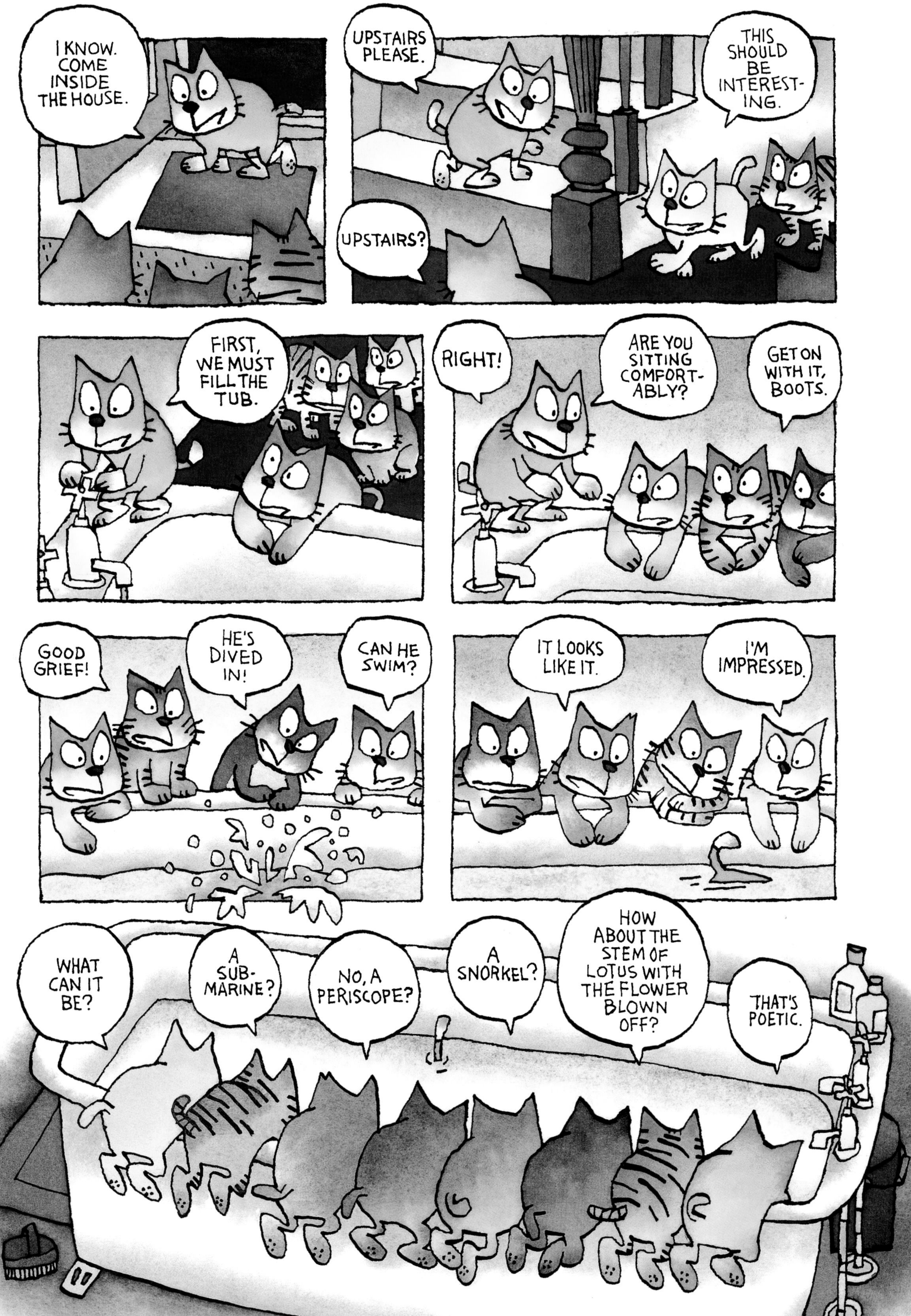
I KNOW. COME INSIDE THE HOUSE.
UPSTAIRS PLEASE.
UPSTAIRS?
THIS SHOULD BE INTEREST-ING.
FIRST, WE MUST FILL THE TUB.
RIGHT!
ARE YOU SITTING COMFORT-ABLY?
GET ON WITH IT, BOOTS.
GOOD GRIEF!
HE'S DIVED IN!
CAN HE SWIM?
IT LOOKS LIKE IT.
I'M IMPRESSED.
WHAT CAN IT BE?
A SUB-MARINE?
NO, A PERISCOPE?
A SNORKEL?
HOW ABOUT THE STEM OF LOTUS WITH THE FLOWER BLOWN OFF?
THAT'S POETIC.

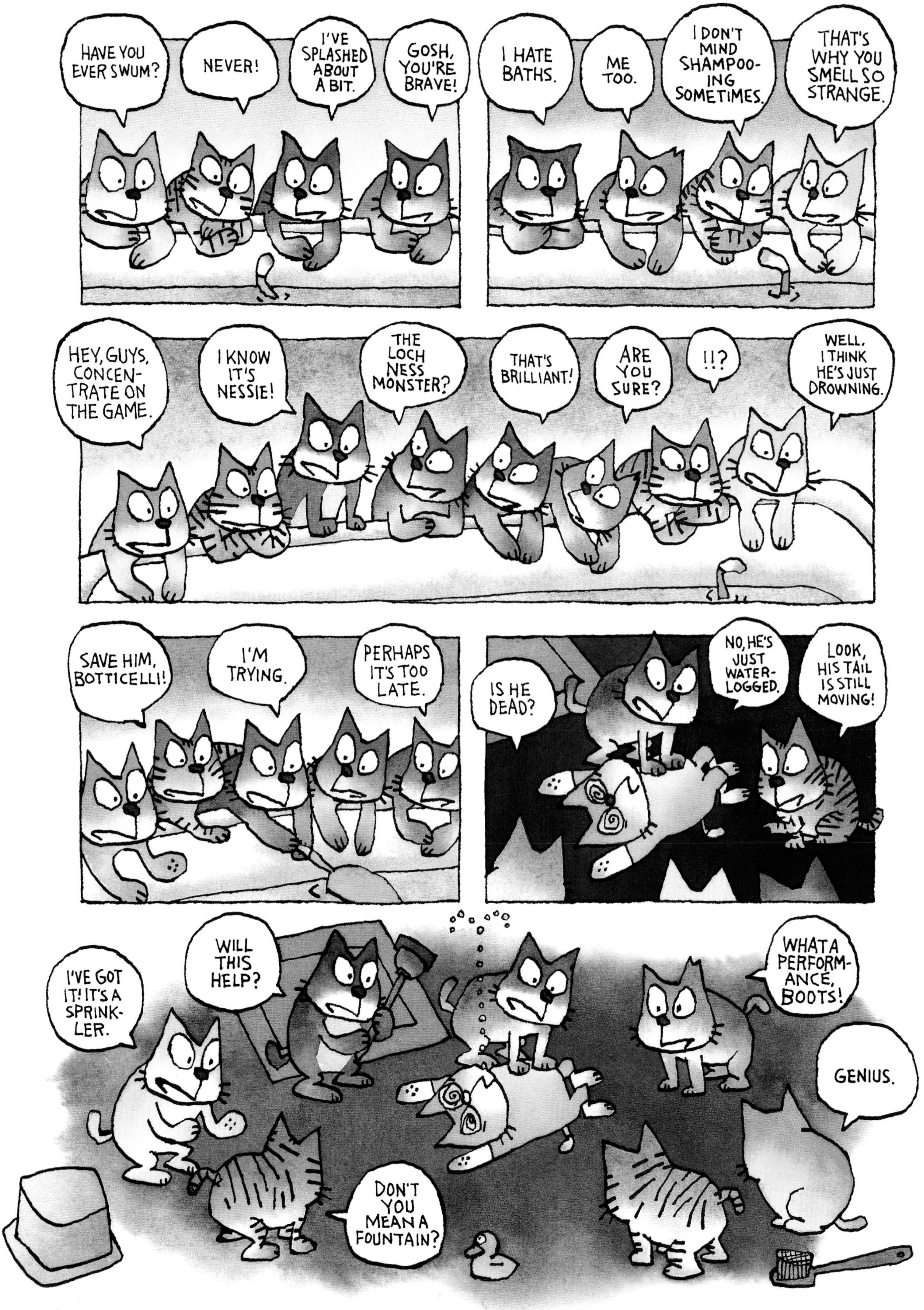

HAVE YOU EVER SWUM?
NEVER!
I'VE SPLASHED ABOUT A BIT.
GOSH, YOU'RE BRAVE!
I HATE BATHS.
ME TOO.
I DON'T MIND SHAMPOO-ING SOMETIMES.
THAT'S WHY YOU SMELL SO STRANGE.
HEY, GUYS, CONCEN-TRATE ON THE GAME.
I KNOW IT'S NESSIE!
THE LOCH NESS MONSTER?
THAT'S BRILLIANT!
ARE YOU SURE?
!!?
WELL, I THINK HE'S JUST DROWNING.
SAVE HIM, BOTTICELLI!
I'M TRYING.
PERHAPS IT'S TOO LATE.
IS HE DEAD?
NO, HE'S JUST WATER-LOGGED.
LOOK, HIS TAIL IS STILL MOVING!
I'VE GOT IT! IT'S A SPRINK-LER.
WILL THIS HELP?
WHAT A PERFORM-ANCE, BOOTS!
GENIUS.
DON'T YOU MEAN A FOUNTAIN?

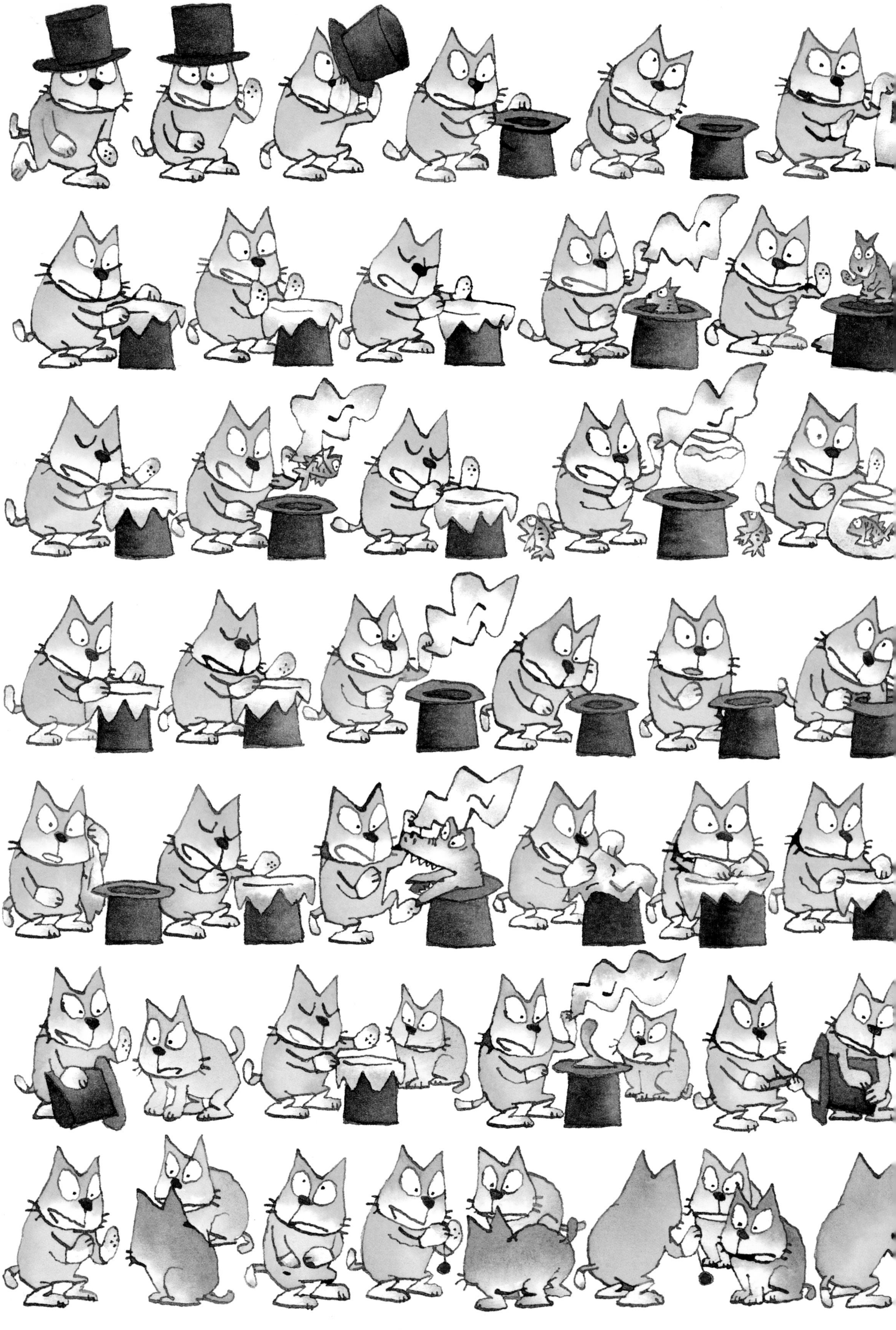

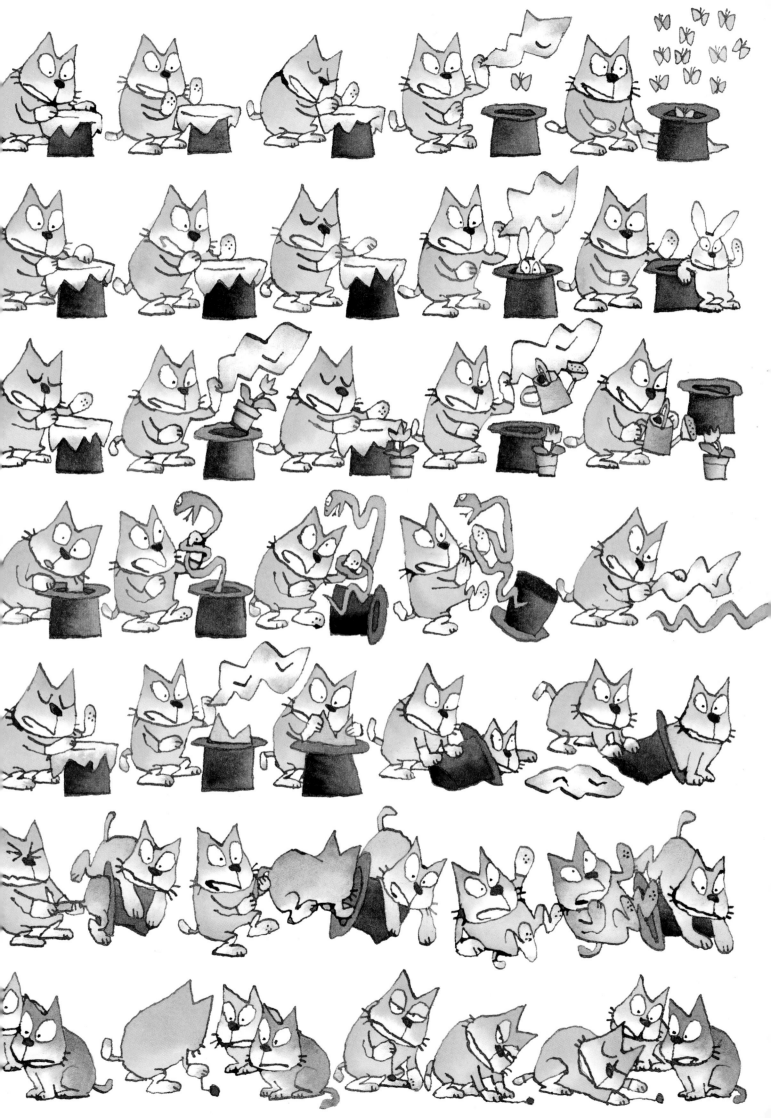

Other books illustrated by Satoshi Kitamura:

HIAWYN ORAM
SATOSHI KITAMURA
IN THE ATTIC
9781849392983

WINNER OF THE MOTHER GOOSE AWARD
Angry Arthur
Hiawyn Oram
Satoshi Kitamura
9781842707746

UFO DIARY
SATOSHI KITAMURA
9781842705919

Me and My Cat?
SATOSHI KITAMURA
9781842707753

Once Upon An Ordinary School Day
Colin McNaughton
Satoshi Kitamura
9781842704691

Millie's Marvellous Hat
Satoshi Kitamura
9781842709481

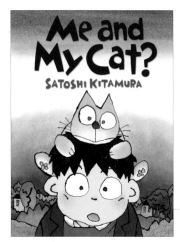

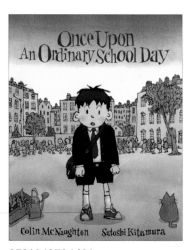

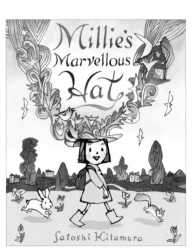